GLIMMER

Editor: Dave Margoshes
Cover art: Sue Bland
Book and cover design: Tania Wolk, Third Wolf Studio
Printed and bound in Canada at Friesens, Altona, MB

The publisher gratefully acknowledges the support of Creative Saskatchewan, the Canada Council for the Arts and SK Arts.

Library and Archives Canada Cataloguing in Publication

Title: Glimmer : short fictions / Steven Ross Smith.
Names: Smith, Steven, 1945- author.
Identifiers: Canadiana (print) 20220213208 | Canadiana (ebook) 20220213240 | ISBN 9781989274705 (softcover) | ISBN 9781989274712 (PDF)
Classification: LCC PS8587.M59 G55 2022 | DDC C813/.54—dc23

radiant press

Box 33128 Cathedral PO
Regina, SK S4T 7X2
info@radiantpress.ca
www.radiantpress.ca

SHORT FICTIONS

GLiMMER

STEVEN ROSS SMITH

who
in this
shadow quadrant
is gasping, who
underneath
glimmers up, glimmers up, glimmers up

–Paul Celan

DECEPTION: A NOVEL

As you form the intention of reading and pause before the bookshelf, you confront a host of possibilities and once you choose, a novel in this case, the novel itself is the first character you meet and you agree to accept that character, a character full of him or her self and not without reason as she is all-powerful, containing and controlling what is revealed or hidden and defining the process of your path through the labyrinthine depths, a path at times clear and in motion and at other times static and perplexing, and on this occasion the novel leads you to a library with unending rows of shelves of thousands of books and you wander there full of anxiety caused not by the ache of loneliness but by the vast store of knowledge which, no matter where you begin nor how fast you read, can only be penetrated to the shallowest level, barely skimming the surface even if you choose only books with near-identical code numbers insuring related content or authorship because with every book you read the list of the unread grows and how can you bear the weight of ignorance and keep pursuing knowledge that is found between the covers of books especially since you've become uncertain whether this is a real library or just an image in a dream or story and so where does it begin and end, before or after the novel you have decided to read and which speaks to you now clearly and perceptibly from these pages, wearing a pair of glasses and a pencil over the ear or a brown tweed jacket with an indecipherable lapel pin or blubbery lips seeping a citric breath and knowing better than you what you're looking for until it occurs to you that it doesn't matter, that you can give yourself over to this tale, that you can follow it regardless of costume, trait, and gender, through representations of dream or reality or plain illusion because you are willing and there is nothing to fear as this is a place where your body is safe, yet you sense that your mind could be endangered though it is you who chooses, pulling down the book that attracts you by its red spine and yellow letters spelling out the words *Deception: A Novel* because you admire the look and you like the way the object feels in your hand, its fullness promising something you long for—a conversation, a journey, an affair with an elegant face, a hat cocked over one eye, a world-worn complexion, a nervous smile, a mouth full of words that tongue into you in the first embrace.

THE CLOSETS OF TIME

—

One Island Morning
Soon, in the distance, a siren will wail.

—

Blanche
The lean, frail woman clutches the railing and works her way down the stone steps beside her house, toward her swimming pool. She's bent forward. Her knuckles are bony and white. Beads of sweat break out on her forehead, wilting the bangs of her grey hair to hang flat and limp. Her arms shake as she uses all her strength to hold herself up and edge, one foot at a time, reaching toward each next and lower step. Moment to moment she relies on, and fights the pull of gravity. The pain in her deteriorating spine feeds her body's wish to crumble.

"Goddam! Come on Blanche." She wills herself on.

A slight cool breeze buffets the early morning air, light just breaking through the trees. Blanche shakes and shivers at the same time. Her bright red robe clings or folds open in the wind's flutter and in her struggle. Her nightdress, glimpsed beneath, is pale green, thinning with age.

In her concentration, it seems as if the whole world, all of her life, closes in, becomes only the few square feet her body occupies, and the push to get her right foot to move a few inches. Just one more step to be close enough to reach for the walker.

She urges her foot to move forward, but something inside her resists— her body at war with itself and her will. Time has brought her this.

She's tiring. When the foot moves over the edge of the step, her leg will be hung in space and all her weight will be poised on the left leg—will it hold? Perspiration and tears merge at the corner of her eyes. She grits her teeth against her fear and her quavering.

Her toes, then her foot's arch and finally her heel move past the lip of the step. Momentum is gained, then gives. Forward Blanche lurches, plunging, crumpling, reaching. She feels in slow motion. Time dashing, time braking, all in one tremulous moment. Time rattling her bones.

—

Roxy

"I'll get those fuckers. I'll get them out of here."

Among the trees, night's dimness lifts slowly in the dawn. Roxy moves like a shadow, but deliberately, with intent.

"This is mine, my sanctuary, my place to escape that sonofabitch." Did she speak these words or did they flash like a familiar headline in her mind? She pauses and listens but there is no trace or echo of her voice in the air. Her face is pale, her eyes dark. Roxy holds the red and black can with both hands, squirts barbeque fluid on the pile of wood scraps—plywood triangles, short ends and shavings—by the corner of the building. It's the skeleton of a cabin, with standing timber and cross-beams, milled from trees felled to make this clearing. Window and door frames are roughed in, plywood floor laid. The structure and the pile of scraps is also close to the stack of lumber waiting to be applied as siding and finishing boards, and not far from the camping trailer. She turns and fires a few squirts in the direction of the stack, careful not to splash onto her black runners or grey pants.

She begins to hum softly, a flat indiscernible melody, but with determination in its lilt. So absorbed is she, that the soft hooting of the owl in the nearby stand of maple goes unnoticed. But a car scooting up the gravel road at the end of the long driveway causes her to stop, to stand stock still until she is sure the sound is receding.

Turning back and aiming higher, she sprays a blast of fluid directly onto an upright support post.

"Hmmmmm-mmm," Roxy hums, now with an attitude of reverence.

In her skin she already feels the familiarity of fire, its inviting warmth, the thrill of its gyrations. She mouths the lyrics now "Don't play with me, m-m-m, playing with fire." She reaches into her bag, slips the fluid container in, and pulls out a yellow butane igniter. She clicks its trigger a few times, until a small shaft of flame, orange and blue, pops out the end of the short black barrel.

Her humming stops, the soft hiss of the lighter her new music. She watches it, listens, then licks her finger, passes it through the flame.

"Now to turn back the clock," she whispers. "Goodbye to your sawing and hammering, all your fuckin' noise."

She lowers the igniter toward the wood scraps. There's a *whoosh* and a ball of orange flame.

She backs away, watching to make sure the fire takes well, then turns and walks slowly up the grade, pausing now and again to look back. The flames lick their red and orange tongues, hungry and bright, upward from the ground, enveloping the beam, illuminating the clearing, as if to rush the dawn. Roxy fades into the forest's shadows and disappears as if she was never there.

—

Bernard & Tina

On the cabin porch, Bernard sits, leaning on the hard pale tabletop. He likes to watch the dawn here in the forest, away from technology and distraction. Sun begins to peek through the silhouetted trees. In the play of light and shadow, sunbeams lift foliage here and there into distinct visibility—the maple's autumn-yellow leaves, the cedar with its flat green needles.

He hears the car brake in the turn-around, the engine shut off and the car door slam. Tina walks up the slope past the perky salal bush, back from the high bluffs where her cell phone could connect.

"There's no use," Tina calls from the driveway. "She said *stay away*, and hung up." Tina disappears behind the thick tree stand. Her words droop in the air.

With the sun's movement, the light shifts to the bark of the towering tree Bernard calls *precipitous fir* because of its sky-reaching height and its off-kilter lean. In a crevasse in the aged tree's scaly bark, a ray spotlights an insect wing caught and fluttering, as if given a second life. A raven croaks somewhere overhead.

"That's unfortunate...very sad." Bernard shouts his words in the direction of Tina's voice, continues, "She's shocked. She'll come around."

A tear glints on Tina's cheek as she comes into view.

"How soon?" she asks.

"Can't say...eventually, I guess."

"She's my daughter. I can't wait that long."

Bernard is aware of the pressure of his elbow on the table, his temple resting on his fist, his wrist cocked, forearm straight and transmitting the weight. His shoulders ache from yesterday's wood chopping. He shifts.

Tina's footsteps crunch on the underlay of sand and stone, seeds and cones.

Bernard had been trying to determine if the old tree is a Douglas or a Grand fir. Not so easy for the untrained eye. It had not been important until recently. And now in his hand, a cone, dropped from one of the branches three or four stories above his head, reveals the telltale mouse-tail peeking out from under the cone's scales; or as it says in the field guide on the table: *the three-forked bracts resembling a mouse's feet and tail.*

"It's a Douglas," he says, as Tina disappears around the corner of the cabin. He hears the door open and close, her footsteps moving closer through the cabin, until she walks through the open screen doorway to the porch to sit opposite him at the table. Her hair is auburn and tousled, her brow furrowed. Her gaze looks not outward, but in.

"I thought when she and I found each other everything would be okay," Tina says.

"There's been that thirty-three year gap," Bernard replies, straightening up and stretching his hands over his head, flexing his shoulders. "Lotta water under the..."

"And she's furious now at me for that, for letting her go. But I was a teenager. I was unfit."

"You shouldn't..." begins Bernard.

Tina interrupts again. "I wish I could go back, fix what happened then."

"How could you? What you did was best." He reaches his fingers across the table to rest on the back of her hand.

A sudden breeze comes down the slope behind them, as if sneaking up, and despite their distraction, its swoosh and pulse catches their ears and carries their gaze to the sway of the tall trees and the shuddering leaves. Bernard adjusts his reading glasses, peers over top of them.

"Do you ever think about this tree here, the Douglas fir?" he asks, tilting his head in the tree's direction.

"Just about whether it might fall on us. Might be a good thing."

"It won't do that, it's our guardian."

"How do you know?"

"Look at it—this old tree, its patience. Standing, growing, waiting, even breathing for us, and doing it all so slowly, with such majesty. There's a lesson there."

"Screw the sappy metaphor. Next you'll be hugging that tree...instead of me."

"Tina, she'll come around. Don't push. Give her time." Bernard rises, moves toward Tina, and with his arms embraces her deep sadness. "Let's talk about it more when I get back from the bakery. I'll bring a treat."

—

Honey & Dean

"Stop! Stop! It's now!!" Honey, stiffening, breathless, in the seat beside him.

Dean stops the pick-up on the edge of the narrow road, the grass there just beginning to lighten in the dawn. Honey's head tilts back on the headrest, her throat is white. He can see her pulse there, rapid in a vein.

"Shit," Dean says, "what'll I do?"

"Help me." Her knees pulsing in and out.

"Can you hang in until we get there?"

A low moan from deep her chest; head side to side.

Dean leaps from the driver's seat, runs behind the truck, pulls a blue tarp from the box, jumps over the ditch and spreads it on the narrow strip of grass between the ditch and fence.

"Here," he says, taking her under her arms and guiding. He helps her ease down onto the tarp, runs back to the truck, reaches in toward the steering wheel, honks the horn madly.

Honey twists, her body locking and releasing as her back arches. Her fair shiny hair spreads, a writhing halo about her head, her fingers clutch the tarpaulin. Dean rushes back to her side. Her skirt is up over her knees, her legs splayed.

"Pull my panties off," she gasps, "it's...it's..."

He pulls at her underwear but it catches on her sandal. With a yank, shoes and panties come off, are thrown to the side. Dean runs back to the truck to honk some more. Then back to her.

"Okay I'm with you Hon," Dean kneels, panting.

They hadn't planned it this way—well not any way. But it was a glorious night that led to this. Celebrating their first year of dating with wine and crackers and brie at the beach under the wide arc of stars, and no one else there; the gentle, constant push of the ocean onto the sand and stones creating a crystalline melody. They sang and slow danced to lines they could remember from "In the Still of the Night" by the Five Satins. Then, snuggled into their two sleeping bags, zipped together, they cuddled, clutched, stroked and gasped, gushed giggles, laughter and tears, on the thin strand between the trees, the sky, the salty sea. They hung on a thread, the thin miraculous fibre of human existence in communion. And the lifelines that were each of them became deeply entwined in finger traces, tongue caresses, pulses of skin surfaces, all moving as one. That night, on the cusp of eternity, the universe sang though their bodies. They changed the course of history—at least, their own.

This morning, that universe has narrowed to a square of tarpaulin and Honey's shining, globular belly, her body's firing up, its spasms and contractions readying to deliver new life. In multiple.

Dean's pulse races, his hands are uncertain, his mind a dazzle of confusion, but he's enraptured by Honey's beauty, and her pain. He runs his fingers through his sleep-ruffled hair.

A car pulls up. Dean recognizes Bernard, a neighbour.

"What's up?" Bernard steps out, around the front of his van, looks from Dean to Honey, nods, says "Honey," cordial despite the circumstances.

"Her water broke." says Dean.

"You call the doctor?"

"The cell won't connect. We thought we could make it. The first one is coming now!"

Bernard speaks rapidly. "The first one? You mean twins? I'll go get the Doc, okay?"

"Hurry."

Bernard rushes to his van, slams the door and peels away.

"You okay Honey?" Dean tries to sound comforting. His heart thuds against his ribs, pounds with the moment's impossibility, its wonder.

"Uh-huh," she says exhaling, her mouth widening. Dean looks at her face. An intense energy—strained and courageous—that Dean's not seen before pulses from her cheeks, her eyes, her forehead. His left hand waits between her legs; he reaches the other to rub her belly.

"Take a deep breath...gently...the baby's coming. I'm here. Lots of time. We'll be fine." His waiting hand shakes.

Honey nods, emits a small smile, and begins to breathe slow and deep, her whole body one focus, on fire, contracting.

—

Blanche

A shaft of pain shoots through Blanche's hip, the corner of the step digging in. Her arms angle up, as in her crumpling—her pelvis and knees giving out at the same time—she'd managed to grab the rail and land on her backside. She feels a cold sweat and can see the cloth of her robe quiver with her trembling. Her face ashen white. Moisture rolls down her cheeks, collects in the creases of her neck.

"Nghghghmn." She sighs and moans, letting the pain escape from her chest and lips like a rush of wind in a veil. Her world spins. She stays sitting until her head clears and the shaking stops.

She sees blood on her knuckle. Her housecoat and nightie are pushed up revealing her sagging thighs.

"Damn! What now?" she wonders. She remembers how she used to bound down these stairs, swim lengths every morning, year after year, right here in this pool.

A feeble "help" feathers from her throat as if uttered by someone else. Then silence. A deep breath to the bottom of her pain makes her wince, stirs her determination.

"Today is not for frailty," she whispers.

The water of the pool is still but for a slight chuff across its surface where the breeze buffs it. Here and there a few rays of sunlight gleam. The sea-blue liner of the pool absorbs both the light and the darkness, making it seem as if there is no limit beneath the surface, making it look like a sky or a bottomless opening to another dimension.

The water's glimmer appears to be winks and nods, beckoning. *Come on. Come Blanche. You can make it.* Calling her to slip into the water and be released from her body's weight.

She pushes with her arms, pulls with her heels, slides her hips bit by bit toward the calling water, its promise. Its promise of release.

—

The Siren

In the distance the wail of the siren calls the volunteer firefighters and medics into action. The wail rolls across the island's hills and meadows, up the steep slopes toward the sky, down toward the streams and low-lying swamps. It rolls along the paved and gravel roadways, nudges through trees and scrambles over rocks, moving outward, uniting everyone on the island through their ears. Everyone stops for that brief moment to look off, eyes tilted slightly upward, concerned, wondering. Everyone strains to hear the real message of the whining siren, a message singular and without embellishment. Yet to every pair of ears, the siren brings a reminder of mortality, a brush with disaster, the knowledge that something close and unfortunate is unfolding, and that next time it could be for them. Then comes the long silence that builds with the siren's fade. But soon it is jabbed by a car engine starting up, or truck tires speeding along a gravel road, or a shout that echoes. Everyone is thinking "I hope," and the thought fills with their own concerns and wishes for the safety or protection of someone or something, for a bit more time, for a normal, or even an extraordinary day.

—

A DANGEROUS COIFFURE

In a salon a woman sitting under a hair dryer opens a sensational tabloid and reads a headline *Aliens disguised as hair dryers feed on human brain cells.*

HAMMOND AT THE BLUENOTE

—

Dear Karl,

Wind gusts knifed blades of cold air through my coat flaps, up my sleeves, and jabbed dust motes into my eyes. Lisa and I were on our way to the Bluenote for John Hammond's one-night-only gig before he moved on to Saskatoon. Maybe that unexpected wind was a premonition, but I didn't know it. The burly doorman insisted we check our coats. I felt we were in New York City where another practice lets them take you for another dollar. I protested. My jacket was just a light windbreaker. He insisted. My mind searched for the logic of compulsory coat checking. Maybe people don't fight when their coats are checked. Or they can't sneak in their drugs or booze flasks so easily. Perhaps coats slung over chairs droop onto the floor creating hazards for waiters. We checked our coats. In a moment of compunction, I extra-tipped the attendant, a slim fellow in a loose-fitting tie-dyed shirt and a droop-down moustache, like a character caught in the sixties.

We searched the long narrow room for a good vantage point and crammed into a table dead centre about twenty feet from the stage. People were drinking beer and chatting quietly, greeting friends, ordering snacks, and waiting for the show. A bouffant blonde server in a tight leather skirt paused to take our order. This could have been a blues bar in any city in North America, any white middle-class city, that is. Small square arborite tables with chrome legs, black vinyl chairs, a stand-up bar to the right, stage at one end. I was excited, I'd only listened to Hammond on record and now was going to see him live and close-up. I squeezed Lisa's arm and she gave me that gleaming smile, that squint of her green eyes that made me feel so good. We revelled in music together—it fuelled our love.

The small stage glowed faint red in the subtle wash of dimmed spotlights. A stool sat empty behind two microphones, one at the height for a guitar and one for voice. A waiter passed with a tray full of beer glasses held on this upturned left palm, level with his shoulders. Without really looking, I absorbed his impression as he walked by. I turned to speak to Lisa. Suddenly his image registered. I blinked and looked again, glimpsed the waiter's back disappearing around the corner toward the bar. *Karl, what are you doing here*, I thought, *in a bar, serving drinks, fifteen hundred miles from Toronto?*

He wasn't an exact replica, but it was you, or some aspect of you. Did you know you were doing this? I mean, does the other you know? The publisher of the avant-garde...that you. Does that one know that his other is working a blues bar?

I grabbed the 'Daily Specials' sheet from inside the menu, flipped it over to jot my impressions. I'll copy them here so you can see my thoughts exactly as they came to me that night.

He flickers through the room, carrying a full tray. He has darting eyes, a tight jaw. He's you but he's different. His walk is quicker, less athletic. I wonder if he reads. He looks like he might read Nabokov, but not Burroughs, and I'm sure he's never heard of your heroes Joseph Beuys or John Cage, or even Dave McFadden.

I wonder now how I could have made those assumptions. But we often do this, don't we? Make assumptions about people simply on the strength of a glance. I can imagine him doing taekwondo like you, and I can see you slinging beer. But the edges are different. Maybe that's it. You're both at edges, but on different sides of them. He might be someone who leaves work later and does something dangerous. Drugs maybe, or sado-sex, taunting authority on the Internet, or maybe even using weapons.

He's wearing black pants and a white shirt, with a silver change dispenser on his belt. You wear black and white too. He's shorter than you, and slighter, more wiry, and he moves quickly, like a water spider.

I felt like asking him if he's ever heard of Mr. Bedoya, your character, or if he was familiar with the vocabulary of torture. But I was afraid he'd take it the wrong way—I mean I didn't think he would have known the connection to your book *Strappado*. But then, how many do—read, I mean—to see things through the eyes of words?

Lisa interrupted me at this point to ask what I was doing. I told her and she laughed, seeming to understand, though she's never met you. I pointed him out to her. She nodded, then studied him until he passed out of sight. She said he didn't look like a writer but couldn't say why. I wonder if she'd think you look like a writer. What do we look like, anyway?

He's just behind me now, on the other side of a standing bar. Someone slaps him on the shoulder. He backs away with that stiff-legged jousting move that guys have with each other in locker rooms, moving to avoid the flicking towel, without losing composure. He pops a cigarette package from his shirt pocket, lights up with his lips drawn tight, bottom lip forcing the cigarette to a slight upward angle, hands sheltering the flame. He exhales aggressively. The slapping switches to a friendly posturing, jibing, and strutting. I've never seen you do this, but I can imagine it.

I began to wonder if I was just making all this up. You know, building a fiction around nothing, exercising my imagination. Lisa told me to go on note-making, that if nothing else, there might be an idea for a story in all this. She's practical.

I'm concerned, finding this other you running around, using up energy. This can't be good for you. Where's that energy coming from? It has to be from your reserve. Are you feeling tired lately? If you are whole, this other shouldn't be loose. It's a sign to me that all is not well. That there's some kind of dissociation going on with you. Is that right? I don't mean to stir things up, but this is how it feels to me. Our doubles get away, then there's trouble. When you're feeling low on energy, maybe it's because there's another one of you out there, draining you, appearing in a place like a bar, a place that he can easily disappear from when you get more unified. Or maybe he changes into some other and gets fuel from a new source. Or maybe we ourselves are others.

In his presence that night, everything I thought and wrote down made complete sense. Lisa insists that all this double stuff is just coincidence, that with so many people in the world, some are bound to resemble others. She suggests that you and he may be distant relatives. That could be. Do you have any family here? Lisa says she feels like she's met you now. Here's my final note.

The blonde must be on a break, because he approaches our table to take our order for a second round. When he brings the drinks I ask him his name, say he looks like someone I know. He says he's Jerry Carleton. I ask him if he has any relatives back east. "Just a cousin, a girl," he says. His steely eyes tell me he doesn't want any more questions. He sets down our beers, scoops up our money and moves off without another word.

John Hammond hunched over his guitar on the club's small stage and launched into Eddie Taylor's *Looking for Trouble*, then rolled on, writhing and twisting with the music, light glinting off his wailing old National guitar. A finger slide on his left hand rides up and down the neck. Legs twitching. Voice soaring and growling, the crowd rolling and rocking with him, loving it, bobbing and wiggling in their chairs, whooping and clapping at the end of each song.

In between songs, he told short anecdotes, with his slight stutter, about how he came to the blues in school in Greenwich Village when he was five years old, where—not through his father, absent after his parent divorced—but because of Charity...I think he said Bailey, Charity Bailey, his music teacher...who sang Leadbelly songs and played the guitar and piano and made each kid sing or play an instrument, a tambourine or gong. It was through her that he began to learn the folk blues.

You know Hammond's music, don't you Karl? I mean, if you were sort of here that night, you must. But, when I think about it, I realize that we've never talked about music, always writing and publishing. Well, it was a special night, ending with a version of Robert Johnson's *Preachin' Blues* that blew the place apart. Did you hear John Hammond music in your head that night—Monday the 2nd? That would be proof.

It took us a while to get to the coat-check room, with all the people trying to shuffle out at the same time. As I was helping Lisa slip her coat on, a scuffle broke out in the middle of the bar. The place went silent. It was Jerry and a stringy-looking dude with glassy eyes who looked like he was on uppers. Everybody backed away. Jerry was crouched in a karate or taekwondo position. The dude had a knife. Its blade moved about two feet from Jerry's nose. I broke through the crowd at the same time as the club bouncer. We moved toward the two of them. Our approach diverted Jerry, and Stringy lunged at him. The bouncer and I were on the guy a second too late. Jerry had taken the knife in the side.

He'd looked just like you in that martial art position. That was what snapped me. I thought it was you. You know me, I don't usually jump into barroom brawls. But I had to help, for your sake. Lisa gave me hell later for getting into something that didn't concern me, for letting my crazy imagination run away with me. I don't think she understood. Mind you, I don't either. I mean, you're there and I'm here, and just because someone looks like you...Did you feel any pain that night? In your side? Did you fight? Is everything okay?

The bloodstain on Jerry's shirt was large, just below his left armpit. They rushed him to the hospital.

It was a long time before we got out of the Bluenote. Seems Stringy had refused to pay his bill and then things went from bad to worse. The police questioned me and took a statement along with my name and address, so I guess I'll hear more about this.

I called the club the next day and they told me that the blade had cut close to Jerry's lung so he'd gone into intensive care overnight and then to the recovery ward where he must be now. I don't know when I'll run into him again except maybe in court. You have never met him (can I assume that?) so all this may not mean very much. I'm going to mail a copy of your book to him at the hospital. Maybe that'll close some kind of gap between you two. Anyway, I hope you both keep out of trouble.

Did you think of me that night? Were you drinking beer? Do me a favour—don't take a job in a bar. Just keep writing stories and publishing your magazine. What are your stories about these days? Do you suppose I'm off the deep end? Let me know...about everything. And let's talk about music sometime, okay?

It was still cool when we got outside. The wind had calmed to a breeze that began to settle my adrenaline. Lisa and I hugged together as we walked. A shiver rippled from my gut through my chest and down my back when I realized what had actually happened. It scared me. I held tighter to Lisa. Everything I thought was stable had suddenly shifted, knocked me out of myself, because I had simply gone with Lisa to see John Hammond, and we had rocked, then ended up in somebody else's story.

Regards,
Steven

THE SURPRISE KISS

She kisses him, taking him by complete surprise in the room filled with friends and strangers where a film flashes on a screen and in the film she kisses him taking him by complete surprise in a room filled with friends and strangers who congratulate them breaking up their kiss as she was kissing him taking him by complete surprise in the room filled with friends and strangers where a film flashes on a screen in the corner of a room and in the film she kisses him though they'd never met.

WHAT IS THE SOUND OF SMOKE?

—

When a lovely flame dies, smoke gets in your eyes.

—

It was in a bar I heard it—say in the early '80s, though it was from the '50s, well really from the '30s—it floated through the air and hovered at a round table in a booth with a cushioned bench and wooden chairs.

The lamp hung low, its plume of light defining the circularity. Waves of cigarette smoke billowed through the glow.

A melody of voices, glasses clinking, and deep exhalations.

Mouths functioned as mouths do, opening, closing, breathing, taking in, shaping words.

Intense eyes. Cigarettes held in lips or between fingers.

An intersection of lives and minds. Around a familiar table in a bar, in the '80s, in time's collapse.

I speak of the song, but also of a story I know. The echoes.

In the moments at the table most things were simple, each person simply present. As friends, in moments outside the rest of life. Free from outcomes, at least. Free from surprises. Almost.

Beer moved up and down in tall mugs. Glasses of wine sparkled, held the shine of ruby and straw, and clinked in celebration.

Smiles and gesturing hands.

They were writers, artists, men and women. One of them is Guy. This is his story. But few stories are enacted alone.

A shape lingers by the door, silhouetted by the outside evening light, a familiar shape, a woman's shape. She slowly scans the room.

At the table, smoke trails up toward the lamp, its fabric and wire shade. The smoke a luminous sensual swirl.

Or was the lampshade made of sculpted metal?

Those were the days, I think, looking back. The conversation intense, but who can hear it now?

It's the splinter of a moment that stays in memory—a word, a scene, a gesture. A line, the melody of a song.

One by one butts crushed into the curves of small black ashtrays. Each time, a trail of smoke accompanied by the acrid bloom of ashy stench wafted for a few seconds then disappeared.

From the street, a whining siren.

Five around the table. No, must have been seven. Or eight. And one chair empty. Beside him, on Guy's left, a red-haired fellow, and on Guy's right the empty chair, then a fidgety woman who watched Guy closely. Guy, chin resting on his fist, and staring, distracted, up at the lamp.

The surface of the table, black, smooth, flecked with ash and shifting hands. Paper napkins folded flat or crumpled in a ball.

"Pass the matches?"

I have to make you believe I was there. But was I?

It was poetry. They all thought alike, as alike as unlike can think.

Foam clung to the inside walls of the mugs.

Every mind its own construction.

Animated conversation rose toward the lamp, seemed to grow in the bulb's glow, then dissolve into the room's thick air.

"...too many confessional poems, too many little I's..."

The love ballad reached its final, almost-transcendent crescendo, strung on violins' ascendant chords.

The table was near the back of the bar. Was there a tablecloth?

If one of them had glanced up to gaze beyond their circle of faces and conversation, toward the siren passing in the street, she or he would have seen the wild flashing lights. And the silhouette.

A geometry-growing complex.

The bar called itself a 'bistro.' From French—meaning a small bar or tavern.

The attentions of those who did glance were quickly drawn back to the table where laughter erupted.

I remember now, the table cover was white cloth with a printed-on floral pattern.

"Pound...that great line near the end...how did it go?"

A basket of bread sat at the circle's centre.

The front door, held open for just a minute or so, admitted a breeze that blew all the way to the back, where it swirled around their heads. Guy felt it and looked up.

"But what about...?" The voice trailed off.

Is the recollection accurate? Do the words represent the actual scene, the true configuration of details?

In the swirl, the air around the table gained a sudden freshness.

Guy hears the siren, drops his fist from his chin, lowers his eyes from the lamp to the faces around him, then turns his glance toward the door.

A bowl of nuts, not bread, sits at the centre, on the smooth black—no—on the flowery pattern.

Another siren, louder now through the open door. And the acrid smell of smoke wafts in, stronger than the cigarette smoke smog hovering over the table.

"...the energy of the line, the torque..."

Clink clink. The server empties the ashes into a tin on the tray. Clears a space on the table.

"Nachos coming up."

Is the server a man or woman?

Guy slips a cigarette from the flip-top pack on the table, takes the matches, strikes one, pushes back his chair. The chair feet rasp on the plank floor, draw the attention of a few at the table for just a split second. He touches the flame to the tip of his cigarette and draws a hard breath. As Guy stands, the air becomes agitated, smoke twirls in all directions.

The server dodges Guy's sudden movement, shifts a jug.

Guy thinks of saying *nature calling*, but the shape at the door has a draw stronger than the need to speak. And there are words enough at the table for now.

Hands flash toward the hard chips and soft cheese.

The fidgety girl turns, one hand on the back of her chair, and her eyes follow Guy's movement; watch the back of his tan jacket as his shoulders hunch up toward his long, tousled, hay-blond hair.

He walks through his own smoke.

A few heads nod. The ginger fellow, Red, looks at the empty chair, Guy's, and shifts into it toward the fidgety girl.

"Just for now," he says, to no one in particular, then looks directly at the girl. "Mind?"

Guy hesitates imperceptibly at the washroom door without turning, moves straight toward the front door. At the entrance he pauses, glances back at the table, sees a world in that bubble of light and smoke. He sees Red speaking now intensely to the fidgety one. 'Gidget' they called her, for the behavioral rhyme. His friends in a scene he knows so well. Monty, Jane and the rest. The mugs and glasses dance up and down on angled arms from table to lips, from lips to table. The volume of chatter growing noticeably, their earnest, stirred voices, the familiar timbres, rising over the din of all the bistro customers.

He turns to the door, to her shape gone through it now, her familiar shape—trim, curvy, thick hair down her back—too familiar. And it pulls Guy through the door.

She stands near the curb with her back to him. Her legs are tanned, contrasting with white shorts, black and white top with the deep-cut back, ringlets of dark hair brushing her shoulder blades, taupe sweater over her arm.

He drops his cigarette to the sidewalk, twists the sole of his shoe on it, at the same time calls her name. "Maddy."

She steps away from him, as if startled.

"Maddy. I only have a few minutes. I'm with my friends."

She turns. His stomach tightens at the sight of her face.

"Hi," she says. Her voice with that sound that penetrates him, slightly nasal, with a smile. You might call it cute, but it's not just that.
"What are you doing here?"

"I came back."

"That's obvious. You disappear. You pop up. What gives? What the..."

A siren swells as a fire truck swings around the corner. The sound echoes off the glass-fronted buildings and amplifies. Guy puts his hands to his ears.

Maddy's lips move, her words drowned by the shrieking noise.

"Let's go...inside," he shouts as the siren fades, aware of the hesitation, the ambivalence in his voice, aware he's unnecessarily loud.

"No. Too smoky. I want to talk to you." Maddy exhales heavily as though breathing out the toxic air. Her lips are painted the palest rose-petal-pink.

Guy watches her lips move, the flash of her white teeth. He's often focused on people's mouths. Friends like me have noticed this—his eye line lowering in a conversation—an odd unconscious trait.

"What did you say...I mean before?"

"I said 'I hoped you'd be here'."

"Uh-huh. Why?" A streetcar rumbles past. Guy inhales the smell of the street. Metallic, gassy. Smoke in the air. "Hoped for what?"

"I came looking for you."

"Yes, I got that. But you've been gone six months without a peep." His gaze lifts to her eyes, hazel pupils with gold flecks glittery in the sunlight.

"I had...I'm sorry."

"Not sorry enough to even send me a note. I didn't know where you'd gone. "

"But you knew I wasn't happy...before."

"Yeah, you and your unhappiness—vanished." Guy in dark jeans, open tan jacket, and a white t-shirt enhancing the blue of his eyes. Those eyes follow the trolley along the gleaming tracks as it comes to a halt a few blocks away where red and yellow fire trucks angle across the road, lights flashing.

The bistro door swings open.

"Hey, you all right, Guy?"

"Hi Gidget," says Maddy.

"Maddy. Oh, hi. Haven't seen you for ages. Guy, we thought you'd drowned in the loo. You coming back?"

"Thanks Gidge. In a bit."

"Maddy too?"

"Don't know."

"Let's walk," says Maddy, glancing at Gidget, then turning away.

Cars stop as Guy and Maddy step from the curb to cross the street. The park on the other side beckons with its welcoming green. Maddy and Guy turn onto a gravel path, their shoes crunching the brick-red stones, scuffing up puffs of dust. Along the path's edges, where the shade allows, small white flowers, lily of the valley, poke above broad leaves, and nod in the warm current of summer air.

As they walk side-by-side, close but not touching, the small space between them bristles with tension, with confused attraction. Guy reaches for words. "Did you...are you happy now?"

"No."

"So what do you want?"

"I want...You'll hate me."

"Thin line between hate and love sometimes."

"Thin line," Maddy's voice quavers. "Yes." Her shaky voice hooks him.

Robins flit in the trees, warble exuberant evening songs.

"On my side of that line, Maddy, it was you I wanted, your love. Nobody else. You didn't have to leave."

"I didn't know what else to do." She sits down on the wooden bench beneath a maple tree. "I had too many doubts."

Guy leans at the end of the bench, one foot on the seat's edge, arm on his knee. The air around the bench suddenly stands stark and empty in a web of silence. Maddy stares into the darkening leafy green, Guy toward the ground.

A sudden gust stirs the tree leaves with a turbulent rustle, seems to prod Guy's words. He speaks to the bench's empty seat. "Too many doubts, too much want, not happy, not settled...it was always like that. I didn't understand why I wasn't enough. I didn't understand what you needed."

Maddy gulps in air as a shiver rushes through her body. She doesn't speak.

"I don't know what else to say. Can you tell me what you need right now? I think we've hurt each other too much." says Guy. "We're not getting anywhere."

He turns and walks away from the bench, toward the street. The red light stops him, as another siren-wailing fire truck downshifts through the intersection. He barely hears it.

Maddy rushes up behind him. She reaches for his right hand. Takes it gently in her own and then with both hands moves their hands to his chest. Inexplicable tenderness. Their force fields magnetic.

"What do you want Maddy...I've...been trying to move on."

She squeezes his hand. "You wanted marriage, you wanted family. I didn't, I just didn't."

Guy stiffens, exhales, looks off.

"And now? What do you want Maddy?"

They stand in the middle of the sidewalk, each staring without seeing. People move around them, glancing, the full stream of life flowing on. In the air, the agitation of the blaze down the block.

"Oh, Guy...let's..." She turns and tugs him with her, and they begin to walk in the fire's direction. Her quavering voice, the thick rumble of the city troubles Guy's ears. The fumes made audible.

"Let's what...?" Guy stops, turns to her.

Maddy looks past him, toward the smoke and the cluster of spectators. Her eyes wet, bright, but apprehension, uncertainty push her eyebrows down, narrowing the gleam.

"One more time—why did you come back?"

Maddy squeezes hard, as if she's desperate, needs something to hold on to. Her touch confuses him. His resistance torments her.

Blasted emotions on his face, flushed and lost. Her eyes tearful, full of painful sadness. Both locked in sorrow. They begin to move again. His feet along the pavement on automatic. Her hand curled in his, urging him. The flashing red lights, hypnotic.

"It's the church," says Maddy, as they approach. "How does a church catch fire? It's just stone and glass and..."

Black smoke billows through broken stained-glass windows. Maddy and Guy nudge through the crowd, stop at the strip of yellow tape.

"...Prayers, people's faith, hopes. Up in smoke."

The arm of the ladder truck hovers in the sky, above the flaming roof. The fireman perched at the top aims a stream of water toward the flames. Dark smoke belches out.

"I went..." She wipes a tear from the corner of her eye. "I went to my brother's in Phoenix."

"All that way to get away from me? You were trying to hurt me."

"There's a flower that blooms on the saguaro," Maddy says. "You know those tall cactuses in Arizona. On top of them, like bonnets, small white and yellow flowers grow, flowers that open for just one night and then close the next day, forever. That flower never opens again."

"Uh-huh?"

"I went to the desert to look at them. Standing there, in the heat, looking at them, suddenly I wanted to come back. I...I drove and drove, and when I hit the outskirts here and saw the traffic and the familiar skyscrapers, it became real, you became real again. I got scared. But I wanted to see you, had to talk to you."

"So here I am, all yours," Guy says. The doubt on his face fills her eyes.

"Guy...I, I met someone down there."

Guy's jaw clenches. He lets go of her hand. Steps away.

Maddy's words rush, "Maybe I was trying to...he was very different from you it only lasted a month I couldn't...I had..." She hesitates, turns her face to him, waits until he turns back. She locks her tearing eyes on his. "I'm...I was..."

The heat from the fire grows suddenly more intense. A police officer moves to the yellow tape, and through a megaphone shouts. "Move back now. Everybody, move back, twenty yards."

Smoke on a downdraft billows into the crowd, stings Guy's eyes. He closes them and begins rubbing. People jostle in retreat.

"I was pregnant."

Blinded, and coughing, Guy stumbles on a foot or a curb, reaches for her.

"Was?"

"I was pregnant...it was..." Maddy sobs, her words fading in the noise.

Guy clutches only air, crashes down and the hard cement sidewalk scrapes his palms, his elbow.

He sucks in a deep breath. It takes him some seconds to refocus.

"What?"

Guy steadies himself, pulls up on one knee.

"What did you say?"

He wipes his eyes with his sleeve, searches the crowd.

A siren shreds the air.

He turns around, looks to the church, the smoke, then cranes his sight scanning past the people, the fire trucks, and streetcars along the block toward the park. He thinks he sees her running away. He jumps to the side for a clearer view. He doesn't see her. He turns and turns. An alien cast hovers in the air, a gauzy blur. A ringing in his ears persists.

She is gone.

Guy stands, uncertain which way to go. Dazed, he begins walking back toward the bistro just as his friends bump out the door. He pauses, and from a distance watches them. They cluster in a group for a few minutes, smiling and jousting, until waving they break away in fragments of two and three, and wander off in several directions, into the burning night.

MIGRATION

Piloerections form all over her body, felt most explicitly on her breasts in response to the cold draft but initially triggered by her terror of the man in the black snap-brim fedora who hovers in the crimson doorway across the street, pacing, but never taking his eyes off her while she bends and straightens, bends and straightens, the motions required to paint grey the wrought iron fence, its vertical shafts reminding her of the shape of spears, implements she's seen in cave paintings while doing anthropological research, but more vividly reminding her of last night's dream where a man in a snap-brim fedora performs acupuncture on her to cure her permanent goose bumps with needles which grow progressively bigger and dig deeper into her flesh and finally are spears and she bleeds and bleeds and the blood flow breaks into tiny crimson streams dividing and multiplying and changing direction at every goose bump until they stir and flap and fly along the length of the river, honking and ascending higher and higher and she tilts her head back, craning her neck to look far above the street, the man, the building, until the geese look like spears then arrows then needles, pins, gray or black specks, her breasts tingling all the while at the thrill and the dark specks disappear and she lowers her eyes to the fence whose wrought iron spears she continues to paint, while eyeing, through the crimson shafts, the man across the street, lifting his black snap-brim fedora to draw his cuff across his brow, wiping the sweat that breaks in tiny streams down his face and on his back causing a shiver and the resulting response of his pale skin, rising into hundreds, perhaps thousands of piloerections as he paces back and forth, back and forth, all the while shuddering and looking anxiously up toward the grey sky.

CAMOUFLAGE

The young woman wore her camo hoodie like a badge. It was not army surplus, rather a designer garment whose look referenced the current global attention to war. It suggested guns. Hunting. It fit tighter than the usual hoodie. She was petite, assertively flirting and playful. A matching camouflage ball cap, brim set low to her eyebrows, and her hair, at back, bobbed through the sizing hole, a swirl of shiny brown ponytail, giving her a pert and confident look. She was arm wrestling on the bar with a young beered-up fellow whose slurring words further garbled his German-accented English. Two young men sat on the barstools, one on each side, an array of empty shooter glasses in front of them, cheering the action on. Everyone else was watching too—the bartender, Lawson and I, and a man and woman seated further down leaning on the bar's varnished wood. A man with straggly gray hair rose from the booth beneath a flickering television screen on shaky legs to get a better view.

Indecipherable rap music played over the house speakers. The lamplights, wicker-shaded, over the bar cast mottled shadows, shadows deflected from her face by the bill of her cap. As she grinned, her perfect white teeth set off her oval face and bright brown eyes.

"Fu-u-u-ck." She strained as he began to press her arm down. She fought back, pushing up a few inches, but not enough. He slammed her arm down and she squealed and gasped, then laughed.

Lawson, on the stool to my left, chuckled, said, "Come on girl you can do better than that." She made a face of pain and shook out her arm.

We—Lawson and I—had dropped in for refreshment and conversation after our ping-pong game at the rec centre. We were quite a bit older than the buddies she'd been doing shooters with—in their twenties, maybe thirties. It was getting hard for me, at my age, to judge others' ages anymore. She might have been about twenty-five. The only one older than Lawson and me might have been the fellow who had stiffly departed the booth for a closer view.

The long bar sat just inside the front door and facing away from it toward the row of whisky and vodka bottles and glittering shooter glasses invitingly backlit on the shelves behind the bartender's alcove. On the wall opposite, and over the shoulders of those seated at the bar, were several booths, now vacant. A slow Sunday night.

After the German lad's victory and a bit of sensuous handholding, she began poking her swaying opponent in the chest and abdomen, then batting his ears and laughing. He hunched over to protect himself. Power and submission. I figured they were on a date and this was foreplay. Competitive and sexual.

"You frickin' chicken." She pinched his pectorals and he squealed and rocked then reached toward her and she pulled back, crossing her arms and covering her own chest with her hands.

"Don't pinch me back." She cupped her breasts like two round tangerines, prominent on her slim body, and all eyes moved to her hands.

"My fucking boobies," she said, teasing with faux innocence. Her smiling eyes darted and caught mine and I glanced away. The enticement game was on. The lubricated patrons took the lure too. I looked toward the other woman at the bar. She was middle-aged, with a mauve scarf draped on her neck and shoulder, a touch of elegance. She was stepping from her stool, tugging the sleeve of the fellow beside her. I felt inexplicably embarrassed, watching them depart. Camo-girl's laughter drew my gaze back.

I'd seen such forces at work before—been around, as they say. But I was there to talk with Lawson, so I angled on my bar stool to give him my attention. Well, most of my attention.

The metallic rap throbbed and seemed louder now.

"Ranna," I called to the bartender. "Who's that rapper?"

"Beastie Boys, love 'em. You know they toured once with Madonna," she said.

34

"Didn't know. My age is showing. Thanks."

I turned to Lawson.

"Not my favourite music," He put his hands over his ears and winked.

"What is your favourite?" he asked.

"Blues, "I said, "and Bob Marley, one of the best ever."

"I saw him once in Jamaica," said Lawson, "big concert. It was just too cool. He was magnetic, magical."

I felt envious.

"Oh yeah," he went on, "Love his positive message—*One Love, Redemption Song, Get Up Stand Up*." Lawson began to hum *Get Up*, low but just loud enough for me to hear, and I joined in for a couple of bars.

Camo-girl hugged her game-mate, jumped from her stool and in passing bumped my arm, which I'd hung over my stool's back, so I turned and watched as she moved off, her tight jeans showing a fit and oscillating body as she crossed the pub floor, disappeared toward the restrooms. The German fellow pushed from his stool and stood, wobbly, glaze-eyed and patting his tan, dirt-stained work-pants' pockets for...cigarettes? keys? Still patting, he angled toward the door, bouncing off the frame, one side then the other, on his way out.

Lawson and I turned our attention back to Marley, lamenting his untimely demise, and pondered what his impact might have been had he lived longer than thirty-six years. The conversation spurred a strange kind of reckoning in me—a feeling that our words were a respectful homage, and yet at the same time, were too small a gesture.

"He was a giant," I said. "A living manifestation of spirit, perhaps an incarnation of soul." I felt humbled in his conjured presence for a few moments.

Camo-girl returned to the room and stopped at the far end of the bar, leaning on it to speak to Ranna. One of her shooter pals, the scruffiest one, who looked more than a decade older than her, jumped from his stool and moved in behind her as she leaned her arms on the bar perusing the menu. He leaned in too, from behind, wrapped his arms around her and set his hands on the bar beside her elbows. This left little space between their bodies. He pressed subtly against her, slanting his head to look at the side of her face and make comments close to her ear, beyond my hearing. She laughed and let it be, but seemed to maneuver, to make herself smaller, to retain a gap between them. I turned my attention back to Lawson and my draught.

"She's a strong girl," said Lawson, "She works at the farm with the horses. You know, the one with the red barn and big meadow, where they keep rescued animals."

For a minute I could see her holding a horse's reins, speaking to it, boldly asserting her authority, but with some care in her eyes.

"She does the mucking out too," he said.

I couldn't imagine her shoveling horseshit. She looked so scrubbed, so fresh, with that shining beauty of youth.

"Sunday night," I said with a grin, "must be the night to let loose, horse around with the men."

Lawson laughed and beckoned to Ranna, who had turned from camo-girl and her squeezer and was wiggling her shoulders on beat to the bass-thumping rap and extending her neck like a flamingo.

"Got any Bob Marley on your player?"

Lawson had a soft way of speaking, with a bit of eastern drawl. Something in the way he said *mucking* and *strong*, even *Marley*, the vowels flattening. The Maritimes in his speech.

"Marley, Bob Marley, reggae." His eyebrows shot up and he ran his hands through his thinning fair hair.

"What, you don't like rap?" She grinned. "I'll look." She scrolled the iPod with her thumb. In an instant the thumping stopped and *Is This Love* rolled from the ceiling speakers.

The song triggered my mind, back thirty years, or more, when I was that twenty-something German lad, young, stupid with drink and so pumped with out-of-control Eros that I took any flirtation, or any hope-inducing gesture as a sign, and I just as readily put myself into the game...

The campfire at the lakeside flared. Marley on the boom box, the young woman with the straw hat, who, when we were introduced, had smiled at me, her dark eyes gleaming—in my mind—inviting. A friend of a friend. What was her name? Louisa, Delia...I don't remember. Doesn't matter now. Next day, after several songs and drinks with the others I invited

Delia to go for a ride in the aluminum rowboat to the island to watch the sunset. She accepted with an unusual deferent courtesy, which I took as a sign. At the island I hopped into the water and yanked the boat up so she could step right onto the sand. We sat on a log and I pulled my flask of Irish Whisky from my backpack, and offered it to her.

"Whisky? I'm Spanish," she laughed, "I should be drinking Rioja." She took a sip, and coughed, hunching and bringing her hand to her mouth. I stared at her smooth bare arm and placed my hand between her shoulder blades and patted. She leaned her head back and took a deep breath and stretched her lovely neck, tanned and contrasting with the pale, yellow collar of her light blouse. Rays of sun passed through its fabric, and I could see her shape.

"*Santo cielo.*" She grinned. She seemed to glow. She was enticing. She was with me. We were alone. I took another hit of the whisky. I leaned so our bare arms touched. Her skin was warm. The sun was low and blazing, fluting the clouds orange-red, pink at the tips.

"Another?" I offered.

She blushed, lowered her eyes, then lifted them again, wide and deep brown, and looked right into mine. We were complicit.

"I shouldn't," she said, but took a tiny sip and handed back the flask. I took a big swallow. The whisky burned as it went down. Heat everywhere—my cheeks, my chest. I reached one arm around behind her, my hand cupped on her opposite shoulder. I lifted my other hand to her chin, turning her face to me and moved my lips closer.

She leaned too and kissed me, quick and polite, then pulled back and stood up. She looked down at me, turned and walked back to the boat. She put two hands on the prow and gave it a light push, enough to put the stern into the water. She got in, sat down, and nodded at the oars.

"Are you coming or will you swim back?" She did not seem angry, just matter-of-fact.

I stared at the sun filtering through a line of trees and edging the sky into soft shades of mauve and deep purple. The boat rocked lightly on the darkening water. Delia, still bright yellow and lovely, waiting, her eyes maybe even a bit apologetic. I got into the boat, shoved us free of the land, gave a couple of hard strokes and felt the rippling water push me to and fro...

The clatter of cutlery turned my head to the other end of the bar. The cook plopped utensils in front of camo-girl beside a plate with a large piece of pie topped with a mound of ice cream. The scruffy pal had moved over to the booth beneath the TV screen, slid onto the bench, and was patting its cushion.

"Here," he said.

"...Sheriff, the Clapton version," said Lawson.

"Uh-huh," I said, unsure, still half in my memory, what I was responding too. Camo-girl picked up the plate and moved toward the booth. The stiff-legged old fellow, returning from a visit to the Keno lottery terminal, intercepted the girl and reached out, and she stopped and hugged him with her free arm and they rocked back and forth, almost dancing, the pie plate, fork, and spoon held in the air with her other hand. They moved apart and she sat down in the booth. The old gentleman dropped in beside her, so they were three in a row with her squeezed in the middle, the bench on the other side of the booth table empty.

I lifted my pint and drained it. Another one appeared as I set down my glass. The German lad, who'd wandered out of the picture after having his nipples squeezed then abandoned, had returned. He came up to us, teetering and with bleary eyes. He took Lawson's hand in a handshake variation and muttered something incomprehensible, indicating a deep fraternal bond. Lawson returned the gesture and their hands dropped and the young man wobbled in place, head turned vaguely in the direction of the girl, but quite possibly without ability to focus in a whirling room.

"What do you think," I asked Lawson, "about camouflage as a fashion statement?"

"What do you mean?"

"You know, its insipid creep into casual urban wardrobe. What's that about? Acceptance of the garb of war? Indifference to killing?"

"Hadn't thought about it," said Lawson.

"I couldn't wear it, in conscience, but the young set seems willing. Did Bob wear camo?"

"Can't recall seeing it on him."

"Now look, on her it's fashion...I'm not a fan...well...or maybe I'm just getting to be an old fart."

Lawson chuckled, nodding in agreement.

The girl let out a squeal. Lawson and I both turned. She slapped at the hand of the presser. He thumped the table and cackled.

"Time to fuck off," she said as she leaned forward, over her half-finished dessert, rose in a kind of crouch, and forced her way out of the booth brushing the chest of the old fellow who leaned back to make room and inhaled sharply. She rushed to the bar and dropped a twenty in front of the barkeeper.

"Thanks Ranna. That should cover most of the bill. *Ciao.*"

Camo-girl had all our eyes—the presser, the old gentleman, the wobbling German, and the two of us, Lawson and me—and as she walked past us to the door near our end of the bar she turned and smiled. Bright and attractive, sure of herself, she bumped the door open with her backside, then whirled and slid into the night, leaving everyone in the bar just a bit more wanting than when they'd come in.

THE BIRDWATCHER

A Merlin sits on the top branch of a barren spruce tree, preening, skreeking, then swivels its head to survey the entire reach of its territory, where it is said it can see a field mouse moving or a dragonfly flitting in the air from hundreds of yards away, while two storeys below a man stands stock-still in the middle of a gravel road, his neck craned back and his binoculars focused on the bird as it fans its striped tail, flexes its grayish shoulders and scapular feathers while the observer, feeling the weight of his own hominid form, yearns to be such a high-perched, keen-eyed, light-weight bundle of bone and feather, to view the tree-tops as his floor and the sky as his limitless ceiling, and his shoulders begin to ache so he lowers his binoculars, tilts his head down, drops to his knees, prostrates himself, unaware that high above, the bird lifts off, circles, eye cast down to where he lies.

FAULT LINES AND STARS

It was not my fault. I was just standing there at the time. Though I read once that this is not an excuse. We are responsible for where we are. That seems extreme to me. Things happen. The sun comes up, goes down. I have nothing to do with that.

Vijay came up. The hill, that is. I had nothing to do with that. I was sitting on a rock, beyond the edge of town, lost in thought, looking over the creek below. The air dry, dusty, with that sharp but musty smell of fall. I was wondering what to do with my life. Well, not my whole life, but about Mila and me, and…It was ever since she took on the mural project, designing and painting the big piece for the side of the building beside the parking lot just across from the café where I often hang out. She'd gotten involved, if you know what I mean, with the project manager. Anyway, that's beside the point. Sort of.

So, Vijay comes up the hill and sees me sitting there. He's puffing, his caramel cheeks tinged red. "Chuck," he says, "what're you doing here?"

"I might ask you the same thing," I say.

"Okay then, what're we both doing here?"

"Coincidence," I say.

"Fresh air," he says, and opens his arms wide, takes a deep breath, draws his arms back and nudges his shoulder toward me, like a fullback plunging for a first down. "See that football game yesterday?" he asks.

"Game for ruffians. I don't watch. Anyway, I wanna be alone."

"Okay, but let me tell you something. It's not worth it."

"What's not worth what?"

"Whatever's bugging you. I know from experience, let me tell you."

"I need to be alone, Vijay."

He looks away, into the distance, then speaks, as if to the universe.

"Is it money or love?"

"You some kind of inquisitor Vij?"

Vijay lets out a small chuckle, turns back, looks me in the eye.

"They're the only two things worth getting hepped up about. Other than finality, mortality, the great beyond." His accent sounds through— slight Hindi mixed with British.

"I'm not thinking about the great void Vijay...well maybe I am...the hole in my heart...or maybe not."

"Well, let me make the void concrete," says Vijay. "Let me tell you. I was listening to my friend Ahrun, who lost his lover, then went bankrupt. He was saying that one blow was a knockdown, the other was deadly. The only two things that mattered. But you know what he found out?"

"No idea."

"Behold! Ahrun told me, one *you* dies..." Vijay pauses flexes his fingers open in front of his face. "And another identity pops up."

"No way! Dead is dead, no second chance," I say.

Vijay says, "No reincarnation?"

"That's a different thing. You're into the deep issues, Vij, beyond my ken."

Vijay puts his foot up on my rock bench and leans in, his blue eyes intensified by his brown face and radiating compassion, clairvoyance. There is a scent about him that seems to me exotic, musky, like nutmeg. His voice softens.

"Chuck, what's eating you?"

I look down at his scuffed and dusty hiking shoes.

"Not eating me exactly, just needing thought. Hard to explain. I'd have to go way back, Vijay."

"Go ahead. Go back as far as you want."

"No point. I *want* to be alone." I shift on the hard rock that digs into my backside.

"Sure you do, but you don't really," says Vijay.

"Really? Oh yeah, you're a psychic."

"Start at the beginning Chuck."

"That's birth. Man, that'd take too long. And anyway, it was not my fault."

"Never is."

"Vijay, you're wearing me down."

"Good," he says, bringing his hands together, palm to palm, resting them on his thigh, and leaning even closer. His voice quiets, almost to a whisper.

"We're in this space together right now. You can trust me."

"I don't know what to trust, but okay, okay, here goes. I took some time off work. It was compensation for the ridiculous amount of overtime I'd put in the last few months. Mila's always out, working at her studio or somewhere. I was spending lots of time at the gym. I met this cute Aussie. Really bright. Fit. Funny. Janelle. Somehow, can't remember how, but we got to spotting for each other with the weights. Well, you know, one thing led to another."

"Always does!"

"Well, not..." a flush of heat rises on the back of my neck. "We both kind of held back once we felt the force, to keep it just friendly."

"But the force was with you, ha-ha-ha," chortles Vijay.

"Vij, this is serious, real, not some movie."

"Just trying to bring a little levity. You know," he stretches his palms out to each side, "perspective."

"Anyway, I must have been acting funny at home, because Mila started asking me 'What's bothering you?' I avoided answering."

"Was that successful?"

"Depends."

"Always does. A conundrum, eh?"

"That's why I'm sitting up here on this hill, trying to think things through...on my own."

"Good idea Chuck. Sometimes that's what we need. A little contemplation."

"Yeah, but when I contemplate it, I get mad, then confused. I'm trying to get past it. You see, I was just standing there, on the corner, just out of the café, looking at the wall where Mila's painting was going to go. I was imagining her working, the sharp chemical odour of her paints, what the painting might look like. And suddenly there they were, Mila and the project manager, name's Andreas, arms around each other walking across the parking lot. Right out in the open. Cuddling. They looked happy."

"Was this before or after Janelle?"

"It was...during...I ducked around the corner so Mila wouldn't see me."

"Aha. But what's this *during* with Janelle?"

"Well, it gets complicated," I say.

"Life, eh?"

"Maybe life and death, like you were saying earlier."

"Death?"

"Figuratively speaking Vijay. Just quoting you. Not death, just surprise, dismay. Mila getting on without me." I put my hands behind me on the rock and lean back.

Vijay, scratching his head, says. "I think I'm missing something here. But I was missing something with Ahrun too. What I couldn't get from his story was what started his plunge toward bankruptcy. He didn't seem to know either. Maybe that's the way it is, we can't see our own hand's role in our own fate. I told him that. He said he had no hand in it, said it was just market forces. I said I didn't see how that could be possible."

"Is Ahrun okay now?"

Vijay sets his foot back on the ground and paces a couple of steps left then right. The grass bobs in the breeze. He is silent.

"Gosh, Vij, I'm sorry. I didn't know Ahrun, but..."

"Yes, it's tragic," Vijay says softly, "Shows you...but too late now...I tried to help him, but talking with him after his crash was like tuning in to ambient music...you know, Brian Eno, *Music for Airports*. All middle. You get lost in it, hardly notice, but you're there, caught in one endless drift. It stops and you don't even realize it's over." Vijay pauses, his eyes lose focus, gaze into another realm.

"Ambient?" I say.

Vijay takes a deep breath.

"Drifting. Unanchored. Despairing. I couldn't reach him."

The wind gusts, stirring dust-swirls. My tongue touches my lips, reaching for a word.

Vijay turns back to me.

"Right then. Where were we a minute ago?"

"Mila and me, but I don't want to burden you further."

"Chuck, we're in the here and now. That's what matters."

"I'm just not sure what that now is, or what to do about it. Don't even know if it matters. Don't know if I can trust myself."

"About what?"

"All of it."

"Well you've got to recognize your own hand in it, in your circumstance, your fate. You can't blame Mila...or Janelle."

"I know...I don't know, but..."

"You do know."

"I'm trying to know."

"Stay with it. That's what I tried to tell Ahrun."

"It's not comfortable," I say.

"Nobody gets guaranteed comfort. But we must...usually...carry on."

"There's got to be more than just carrying on, Vijay. I've lost something, but does it matter? Being out there now, on the loose, I can't trust myself. There's sorrow, beauty, temptation. I'm on a carnival ride. I feel like I fall in and out of confusion, of love, twice a day...with a moment, a smile, you know, Mila, Janelle, Kristy, Cierra, a swish of long shiny hair, the shape of a leg, those bonbons of desire. Mostly just in my mind. But with each infatuation, I feel dizzy, and like something else has to die."

"Ah, desire, the current's pull. The whirl. All flow, and you're alive! We resist. We think it shouldn't work like that."

"How should it work?"

"Love should beget love; desire, desire. Out of control. But things work the way they work, not the way we think we want."

"Like the parking lot. It burned me at the time, and still does...yet it looks small, far from here right now."

"That's good. Not to worry, you'll figure it out. Keep Ahrun in mind. Don't give up."

"I didn't know Ahrun."

"Seems he didn't know himself. And I thought I knew him but didn't." Vijay's shoulders slump. He looks toward the ground. "I wish I had spoken more frankly, more honestly, with him. It might have saved him."

I look past him to the sky. My throat feels dry. My mind is a knot. Neither of us speaks. The sun flickers behind a thin cloud.

"Right then, Chuck, I'll leave you to it."

"Okay...Vij, I'm sorry about Ahrun."

"Thanks, my friend."

Vijay starts down the hill, stops, looks back toward me. For an instant he seems bathed in some kind of pure light. I blink and he looks normal again.

"Let me know, or call if you need," he says, then turns and heads off. I watch him get smaller and lower until he disappears into a grove of trees.

The wind rises up, blows dust into my eyes. I rub lightly on my closed eyelids until the grit dissolves, then I keep them closed. The wind's bluster is all that I can hear.

I sit a while longer, watch the afternoon fade. The air cools. I begin to see that it might not be Mila and Andreas that is my problem. Well, I don't mean problem, but my upset. Well not really upset. My anchorlessness, my uncertainty, my...I don't even know what...and calling it Mila and me is not even right. So what is it?

I make my way back to town, collect my gear, and head for the gym as night falls. If sitting still didn't help me, then maybe exercise will. The gym has mirrors on all the walls. They reflect reality as you perceive it— your physical deficiencies, your assets, where there's room for improvement. As I lift my orange tank top over my stomach for a peek, I can see all of this, with the emphasis on the room-for-improvement category. I have no abs, and my biceps and triceps look soft. I have a slight slouch. What did Mila see in me? If she saw anything. Truth be told, we'd been on the fade for some time. And what delusion am I under in thinking that Janelle is my answer?

No sooner does Janelle cross my mind, than she pops up. She looks terrific. Turquoise tights and lime green top, ponytail crown, strands pluming like a fountain.

"Hi, Chuck. I'm later than usual, so didn't think I'd see you here."

"We're both late at the same time, so I guess we're on time."

Janelle smiles. "Suppose you could say that. What're you working on today?"

"My slouch," I say, pulling my shoulders back. "My posture. Bad genes. All the stuff my parents left for me when they headed on out."

She raises her eyebrows and tilts her head. "I don't think I'm following you."

"Me neither. Just feeling sorry for myself."

She raises a scolding finger.

"That's not attractive, Chuck."

"I know. Guess I fell into a Bob Dylan moment."

"You've really lost me now," she says.

"If you ain't got nothin' you got nothin' to lose."

"You're talking in riddles. I can't tell if you're being funny or sad." She starts to turn away.

"Me neither," I say. I angle toward the pull-up bar. I tilt my head, beckoning her attention.

"Want me to spot you?" she asks.

"That'd be great." I smile. Maybe the first time I feel like smiling—a genuine smile—today.

I put one hand up on the bar and look over my shoulder to Janelle. Her eyes seem extraordinarily beautiful right now, deep aquamarine and kind. I want to tell her that, but instead I say, "I was talking to my friend Vijay today."

"I don't know Vijay."

"Kind of a guru. He said love should beget love; desire, desire. Do you believe that?"

"Makes sense to me. Sounds appealing, love love, desire desire." The corners of her mouth curl up a bit, a hint of flirtation. "Okay, put your other hand on that bar. Go for it, Chuck. Go for more than you think you can do. I'm right here if you slip."

As I look up toward the bar and the ceiling above it, I see the skylight, and the stars twinkling through the glass. I pull up and get just a tiny bit closer to them. The inches feel huge. I think of that as I lift—just inches—six pulls, then two extra, the last two a real strain, and my left hand almost slips off. I can feel Janelle standing just to my side as I lower.

"Awesome," she says.

We switch places. Her hands go up. I'm still puffing as I spot for her. Janelle matches me, six and two. I put my hand between her shoulder blades as she lowers from the bar. She's sweating and her scent is soft, citric. The word *bergamot* pops into my mind, though I don't know why. Through Janelle's thin top, her warm skin, her muscle, I can feel her heart beating hard.

THE UNSATISFYING LANDSCAPE

The saffron moon hangs, its light buttering the bottom of clouds over a glassy lake as two figures hunch on a dock whispering and watching, hearing far off in the forest the *hoo-oo* of a great grey owl, and from behind them at the forest's edge, the boisterous voices of the six others returning from the bar and passing through the art studio where, in a mischievous bent, they search for the painter's unsatisfying landscape which he has turned to face the wall and they hang it up beyond his easel and stand back looking, laughing, imagining his surprise in the morning, and suddenly the lights go out, due, according to their attempts at explanation, to some far-off lightning strike, a failure in the grid, or aliens, and the darkness is a wide throat swallowing everything from view—the landscape, the returners, even a hand in front of a face—and the blackness hovers until dawn breaks and the last edge of night is finally banished with the bell calling people to breakfast, at which six people are missing causing little concern as it is assumed that they are sleeping in, and the painter has already finished his toast and coffee and is heading for the studio where he discovers his landscape painting hanging and in that moment becomes certain that it is a failed piece and so prepares the gesso and begins to apply it as a ground coat over the whole scene, over the lake, sky, and forest, not noticing, in that forest, the six tiny figures waving among the trees as they disappear under his brush, and when the whole surface is covered he begins to scratch with a palette knife the outlines of a night scene where a saffron moon hangs, its light buttering the bottoms of clouds over a glassy lake where two figures hunch on a dock, whispering and watching, hearing far off in the forest the *hoo-oo* of a great grey owl and from behind them, at the forest's edge, the boisterous voices.

REASON TO BELIEVE

Lucky, his suitcase on the bed, is rifling through his dresser drawer and throwing underwear and t-shirts into his suitcase. The radio's playing, slightly off its frequency, *Hey Jude* pushing through the fuzzy sound.

"I had a strange dream, Krupa. There was a dog in it. He was old and brown. Not an energetic puppy like you. You're black and white, eh, not brown? Do you know that? The dog was lost in the city and he had my drumsticks in his mouth. I was looking for him but he was always somewhere else." Lucky talking over the radio. "That dream had me tossing and turning all night."

He pats Krupa on the head, snaps the suitcase closed, lifts it and starts for the stairs. Krupa follows as Lucky sings along with the radio. When he belts the line "take a sad song..." Krupa begins to howl.

Tara, just home from the all-night shift at the hospital, stumbles into the Krupa-Lucky duet and almost trips over the jumble inside the front door. Krupa runs toward her. Lucky, his voice trailing off, stands by the archway to the dining room, black suitcase in one hand, a box of Milk-Bone in the other.

"Tara, I'm heading out," Lucky says.

Tara closes the door and slips off her plum-toned topcoat.

"You look good," says Lucky.

Tara laughs, a half-laugh.

"You always say that on your way out the door." Tara eyes the suitcase. "Another road trip with the band?"

"No band, just me solo. I'm going to L.A."

"Solo? L.A.? Huh? That's big news."

"Yup. I've got to make a change."

Tara throws her coat over the back of the sofa. Lucky sets the suitcase down.

"I've got a connection, a referral. A guy heard me play last week at the Legion, told his bro-in-law agent in L.A., who called me."

"Wow." She pushes a loose wisp of her dark hair over her left ear. "Any reason you didn't mention it before? Or like, call me at work?" Her face flushes red.

"*Wow* is right. He phoned out of the blue. Last night, after you went to work. He wants to see me as soon as I can get my ass out there. So I'm going." His words accelerate. "Look at me, been playing drums around Lethbridge over ten years now for effen dribs. I'm a getting-pudgy-gigging-in-gymnasiums-thirty-three-year-old-playing-for-peanuts-going-nowhere drummer."

"That's a bit harsh, Lucky."

"That's the reality. So, it's now or never!"

"*Now or never*, your mantra the whole year since you moved in. You sure this L.A. invite is legitimate? There must be five thousand drummers in L. A."

"Five thousand and one very soon." The Milk-Bone box rattles as Lucky steps toward her. "If it goes well, I'll stay a while."

Tara steps back. "Stay there? A while? Like permanently?"

"If there's work. If I can get a card."

"What about me and Krupa?"

Krupa looks toward Lucky with his wide grey eyes and lolling tongue.

"You've got a job. And they might not let Krupa cross the border. He'll be more content, more stable here. I don't know what my circumstances will be."

"He'll be alone for a big chunk of the day. That's not good for him."

"Just for a while, then I'll make arrangements. Here, I bought a box of treats. Give him one for me once in a while." Lucky reaches into the box. Krupa perks his ears.

"What're you leaving for me?" Tara's eyes wide, moist, stare straight at Lucky.

"Yeah...I'm not...you know how I've...like I said, I just gotta do it. I'm too unhappy for you or my music. I need to drum with some real pros, with some fire. I need to shape up my chops. I need a challenge, some success. I'm not sure what that means for us, but..."

Tara looks away from Lucky.

"You and me with your drum set in between. Not to mention your dog. It's..." She looks down at the floor, then around the living room. "What about the rest of your stuff?"

"Tar..." her name stops in his throat. "I'm sorry, I'll take care of...I need to do this. I thought you'd understand." He takes another step toward her to make some parting gesture. Tara brushes past him, walks toward the kitchen, right out onto the back porch the door slamming behind her.

Lucky calls, his voice raised, toward the closed door. "I'll be in touch. You should do whatever you need to do...I'll leave some money and will send more for Krupa's food when I get gigging."

He swivels, stuck to his spot, to back door to Krupa to front door to the back door again, its curtains still twitching from the slam. Then he calls out. "I...I'm sorry...I'm going by the studio, but I'll leave the extra key here...Bye Tara."

He pulls out a Milk-Bone, tosses it to Krupa's eager mouth.

"See you boy. Remember the dog dream. Don't get lost."

The dog drops to the scatter rug, crunching the cookie.

"Sorry." Lucky shrugs toward the back door. He sets the box on the counter, digs in his pocket and puts a fold of bills and some coins beside the Milk-Bone, picks up his suitcase, stick pack, and walks out the front door and down the porch steps. He pops open the hatchback of his old navy-blue Volvo station wagon, loads his gear in beside the snare drum, slams the door, jumps into the driver's seat.

About 8 PM, Lucky, left hand on the steering wheel, right hand twirling a drumstick, rolls out of the hills on the Number 15, and begins to slow at the edge of the motel strip of Butte, Montana. Just as he's wondering whether to stop or not, the rear axle bangs and the car shudders. The drumstick flips from his hand and clatters on the dashboard. Back tires bounce and squeal, drum set in the hatch clunks and hisses.

"Fuck. What was that?"

Lucky aims the car for the shoulder, coming to a sudden halt. He squints ahead through the bug-splattered windshield at the Super 8 Motel sign blinking one hundred yards down the road, and the stretch of lights that is Butte, a town, it appears, even smaller than Lethbridge. The car does not move another inch, so Lucky puts on his flashers and gets out to see what the problem is. He walks around the car. A haze of light smoke rises from the underside along with a hot metal odour. He reaches back in beside the steering wheel and pops the hood. As far as he can tell, there's nothing amiss with the motor, nothing he can see. Leaving the hood up he kneels and looks underneath. Just that acrid smell. He stands and waves the sparse traffic by, while figuring out what to do. He leans against the car's bumper and searches on his phone for a tow service.

When the truck emerges from the lights of Butte, it slows, does a U-turn and pulls up behind. Silver letters gleam from the cab's orange door—*Buster's Towing*—and a large paunchy man jumps out, brim-up greasy ball cap on his head.

"Bit of trouble I take it, my friend."

"Rear axle issue, I think. Is there a good garage around here?"

"Best one's Silver Bow Auto. Closed now, though. I can drop the car there tonight for attention in the morning, open at 7 AM"

"I've got gear I need to unload. Rather not leave it out. How about down there to the Super 8. Think they'd have rooms available?"

"Oh yeah, Butte's pretty quiet these days. I can go anywhere. Your call." He pokes the peak of his cap up a bit further. "Seventy-five bucks to Super 8, ninety-five if I have to wait in the lot while you confirm your room."

"Seventy-five to go practically across the effen road?"

"Basic service charge. Hook up and drop. Could be worse, no mileage charge. Discount in the morning if you want a tow to the garage."

"Okay. Deal. I'll phone ahead while you hook on."

Lucky approaches the front desk, interrupting the young clerk's attentiveness to Bob Seger's "Night Moves," emanating tinnily from a small portable radio. Lucky signs in.

Back in the lot, he slips the cash into the driver's work-stained palm, then begins hauling instruments and travel bags to his room. Sitting on the bed's polyester cover, looking at the pale taupe walls and the faux artwork, Lucky feels an unfamiliar flutter in his stomach. It feels like fear, uncertainty, though he'd rather blame it on that sketchy hamburger he ate earlier in Helena.

"Seventy-five bucks lighter," he thinks, "under three-hundred cash left. Hell, I need a beer." He picks up the glossy magazine from the side table—"*Welcome! What To Do When You're In Butte*"—on the cover an ad for a band playing the Flying J Casino.

"Hold me back," he says aloud at the sink as he slaps water on his face. He peers into the mirror at his road-bleary eyes, stubbly chin. His sandy-coloured hair, tousled from driving with the windows open, is just a bit more wild than usual. He runs his wet fingers through it, restoring a semblance of order, and grabs his jacket.

After a few minutes of pacing in front of the motel, he eases into the front seat of the BlueBird taxicab. "Flying J, please."

Soft lighting in the entry and between tables, and bright, focussed lights over the bar to draw customers to its gleam and warmth. Lucky has slid onto bar stools like these before, when things have been going good. He's played what he thinks of as "too many" such venues around Alberta.

"Whatever lager's on tap, please," he says to the blonde bartender, staring a bit too long at the silver stud that pierces her lower lip. He spins around to face the music.

The band is a middle-aged quartet made up of drums and guitars—lead, bass, and rhythm—playing "Midnight Hour."

So familiar. So much of what he imagines he's trying to escape. The room is all frosted glass and warm wood. His beer arrives. He nods and smiles, taps his fingers on the chilled glass, takes a swallow, and turns to look through an archway, to the flashing lights of the electronic slot machines, mesmerized customers perched on tall stools. "Gonna wait 'til the midnight hour" pumps from the bandstand, the drummer singing. Lucky turns back, as the studded server pauses in front of him.

"How's your drink?"

"Dandy." Then he blurts, louder than he realizes, "Might need a few more to get me to midnight. Seems a long way listening to Wilson Pickett light, 'til then."

She turns away.

"Now that sounds like a smart-ass crack."

Lucky flinches, turns on his stool to face the voice on his right. The big fellow next to him scowls.

"You could always go listen instead to the trills of the slots, take a chance on the jangly graces of lady luck." The speaker's forehead wrinkles and his big pale moustache tweaks up on the left side. He points at Lucky with a finger and a cocked thumb, squints as if sighting along a pistol. Lucky nods, a nervous smile. "They're Butte's best, pal," says the moustache, leaning his sturdy bulk toward Lucky. "But rest easy, the set's almost done, tout fini," sarcasm in his tone. "They'll soon stop offending your tender ears."

Lucky pulls his neck into his shoulders, turtle-like, turns his attention back to the beat. The drummer is fluid, holding back a bit, maybe saving up for another tune. Lucky nods back toward the moustache.

"I'm grumpy. Personal circumstances. Tough day. I take it back. Sorry. Band's good, solid."

The beer feels good on Lucky's tongue. He taps his right foot along with the beat, with the set's last song "American Woman." The drummer sways, bops, and leans with the driving rhythm, singing the lines. *Garrett & The G-Tones* scrawled on the bass drum skin that vibrates with every thump. Lucky bobs his head. The lead guitarist, long brown hair, round face, looking uncannily like Burton Cummings without a keyboard, finger-picks a wailing riff, just like the original; the bass player, a tall Black man, hunches at the edge of the spotlight over his long-necked instrument, its tip dipping and rising. Two couples bounce erratically on the dance floor. The music begins its slow fade.

"So mister, you a music critic?" asks the moustache.

Lucky chuckles. "I suppose you could say that."

"You're not local. Can't imagine *Rolling Stone* though, rolling someone out to the Flying J to look for talent."

"You never know," says Lucky, turning away to deflect the conversation.

With a flourish and a symbol crash, the band finishes the song, bows and exits. A flutter of applause.

Lucky's phone buzzes in his pocket. He pulls it out and glances at it— Derek on the display—one of Lucky's sometime band members.

"Not now Bro," Lucky mutters and puts it, unanswered, back in his pocket.

"That your doll calling you?" asks the moustache. "I say leave me alone when I'm on the job. Hell, that's why my cell's on mute, absolutely."

"Ha-ha. No doll. My editor at *Rolling Stone*," Lucky blurts. Spontaneous. Entangling himself even further.

"You don't say. Might have known. Seems we're due for media attention. Been years. Back in '82 we had the national TV media here when the mines closed." He moves his stool closer to Lucky. "Did you see those stories— maybe you're too young, sonny? Interviewed a bunch of us. Munched us into their news-feeds when the Berkeley Pit was shut down. Damn rapacious, those mining corporations. That's what I said. But no big media since that. Ain't exactly NYC here now is it?"

"You've been here a while then?"

Stache pauses, sizes up Lucky. "Depends on your perspective...Einstein's theory of relativity." Stache wags his fingers, like slow windshield wipers. "Been here, been there." Fingers back and forth. "But really now, you don't look like a journalist."

"We come in lots of styles." Lucky forces a chuckle. "Even in disguise."

"Hanging around long?"

"Wasn't planning to. Axle might have something to say about that."

"Axel? Your editor, your axe-man?"

"No, no, my gee-dee rear axle seized up."

"So, you're gathering moss," his raspy chuckle barks through the moustache, "not stories." He turns away, responding to a hand on his far shoulder.

"Garrett. Good set," says moustache, shaking hands with the drummer. "Buy you a drink?"

"Scotch on the rocks. Thanks."

"Cindy, Scotch for my G-man...please."

Lucky shifts on his stool, leans and looks away.

"Take a seat, Garrett, meet my chum, music critic from *Rolling Stone*." Moustache puts his hand on Lucky's arm. "Your name again?"

Garrett reaches his hand.

"Lucky," offering a reluctant handshake.

"Garrett." His grip is firm, pumping up and down, a drummer's habit that Lucky recognizes. Garrett's frizzy dark hair frames a lean face that contrasts oddly with his stocky build, stockier than he looked behind his drum set.

"I should get in on the intros. I'm Stace, and this is my place," says the moustache, grabbing Lucky's right hand. His handshake is horizontal, elbow gyrating, like the connecting rod on a steam-train wheel.

"*Rolling Stone*, eh?" asks Garrett.

"Well, that seems to be the story."

"You writing about us?" Garrett's eyes blink rapidly as if matching a drumhead's vibrations.

"Uh, yeah, sure." Lucky feels heat rise across the back of his neck.

"Anything you need to know?"

"Nothing at the moment. Just listening. "

"Surprise guest's gonna turn you on in the next set then. Maybe you know him."

Lucky's interest is piqued.

"Who's...?

Stace steps off his stool. "Garr, we got some business backstage."

"Who's the surprise?" asks Lucky.

"Wouldn't be a surprise now would it." Garrett blinks, raises his eyebrows, drains the glass of scotch, ice cubes and all, follows Stace.

—

Tara paces the living room, then stops, looks at Krupa lying with his jowls flat on the rug, his eyes following her every move.

"Don't look so forlorn, Krupa." The dog blinks.

Tara moves some of Lucky's piles and boxes from the floor to the table to the closet.

"We have to get over this. Looks like just you and me from here on."

She clutches some sheaves of sheet music, stares at them, then tosses them into the black garbage bag.

"Just you and me."

She yanks the plastic ties tight on the bag's neck.

—

"Ladies and gentlemen. We're thrilled to invite a special guest to the stage right now." The band flourishes a short crescendo. "All the way from Chicago, the one and only Buddy Guy."

Lucky turns so quickly on his stool that he almost falls off. "Can't be!" But sure enough, there he is ambling onto the stage, sunglasses, cocoa-coloured fedora, the band easing in to "Hoodoo Man Blues." Buddy Guy, in a casual voice, saying how glad he is to stop by and play with some old pals. Lucky scans the room and tries to comprehend. The band amps up and Buddy slings his guitar from his shoulder, slides a metal bar over the strings, up the neck, and the instrument begins to moan.

Lucky's body goes one way and his head another. His body pulsing with the beat and Buddy's amazing guitar; head scrambling to make sense of Buddy Guy, right here, right in front of him, in the Flying J Casino in Butte, Montana.

"I must be hallucinating," he thinks. "Tara'd never believe this," says Lucky, half to the air and half to Stace. A guitar flourish snaps Lucky's attention back to the stage. Patrons stream toward the dance floor drawn by the pulsing beat, the wailing guitar. The room's energy lifts and flows. The slots, the felted tables, unattended. Heads bob, knees bounce, dancers wave their arms and spin; people nod and smile at each other through the rhythms of the songs and a beat that keeps driving. The joint jumping with the primal joy that intense, energetic music generates.

"Sweet Home Chicago" belts into the room. Lucky turns to Stace, sitting steady with a big grin on his face, his meaty hand bouncing on the bar. Lucky nods and turns back as Garrett's drum snaps the song to a slashing close.

"Buddy, Buddy Guy. Let's hear it," shouts Garrett into the microphone. Hoots and applause. Buddy slings his guitar back behind his arm, his hand gripping the neck by his side, and he steps from the stage into the audience, weaves through the crowd and tables, brushing and shaking hands as he moves toward the bar. He reaches Stace, gives him a cool low five.

"Great show Buddy buddy, I owe you now," says Stace.

"No-o-o brotha," Buddy says, slow and easy, grasping his hand, "we're well even Stace my man. Easy stop en route. My pure pleasure."

Lucky, speechless, leaps off his stool and offers his hand. Buddy shakes it, smiles, and turns away.

"Rockin,' thanks!" says Lucky, finally finding words, said to Buddy's back as he moves to the door. The G-Tones are playing again but to Lucky their sound seems distant. He turns to them, then as if awaking from a reverie, he rushes toward the exit, in time to see Buddy Guy step into a touring bus, the door closing behind him. Lucky waves spontaneously as the bus signals and merges onto the roadway, pulling something in Lucky along with it, something aching in him, the moment so great, so powerfully musical, so brief, so gone. Lucky yanks out his phone and autodials Tara. No answer. He stares a long time at the bus's receding taillights as they diminish down the highway and fade into the night.

Back on his barstool, Lucky orders another lager. "I can't believe it, Buddy Guy here, playing with the G-Tones, in Butte, Montana. That was glorious."

"Believe it man. You saw, you heard, you shook his hand. Reason to believe," says Stace. "You've never meet Buddy before?"

"No, never. Seen him play, but..."

Cindy, smiling, places the draft of beer on a coaster in front of him.

"I'da thought you woulda, being a critic and all. Music's a small whirly world."

"Sure is Stace, but, I'd..."

"I used to tour with Buddy, hit the road with Buddy. We go back. Led the brass when he needed bad-ass horns in the band—until the damned arthritis stiffed up my hands."

"No!"

"Yup."

"So that's why he's here?"

"Passing through, the man's on his way to Portland. Then he'll rattle Seattle then cruise up Vancouver way."

"Listen Stace...is Stace short for something...Never mind...I'm not a *Rolling Stone* writer. That was just a joke. You sort of started it anyway."

Stace stands off his stool. "Hells-bells, you a liar then, a con?"

"No, just a drummer." Lucky takes a swig of beer.

"You mean that figuratively, like marching to a different...or, like, musically?"

"Like Garrett."

"Shit man, why'd you hit me with a lie?"

"Long story pal. Main issue right now isn't my chops, it's getting my axle fixed."

"So, you a pro drummer?"

"Uh-huh, it's my job...when there's a job."

"You going to a gig?"

"Lookin' to better my opportunities. On my way to L.A."

Lucky steps from the stool's rung. "Time to go. Big driving day tomorrow. Nice meeting you, Stace."

"Whoa, Lucky. You're in the biz, I'm in the biz. Still beer in your glass. Let's hear a bit more about you."

"Not that much to tell, sir. Comes a point..."

Garrett strolls up. "Some set, eh?"

"Fabulous Garrett. Congrats," says Lucky. "You guys were cookin'. Must have been a thrill." Lucky downs the last of the beer and slips on his denim jacket.

"Indeed, Buddy's awesome. Always a treat to play with him. Stace's connections do the trick."

"That's cool. Sure as hell surprised me" says Lucky. "Here's my card, Stace, in case you're ever in L.A., or maybe up in Alberta...if I go back there. I know that scene, such as it is." Stace fingers the card, a graphic of a snare drum with a pair of sticks at rest beside his number and name. *Lucky Levitt, Rhythm Ace.*

"Here's one for you too, Garrett. By the way, your beat was solid. Good to meet you fellas. Wish me luck. Au revoir."

"Okay, Lucky Levitt, son of a drum. You runnin' to? Or runnin' from? Adios."

Lucky bumps out the door and takes a big breath of the cool Montana night air.

An early morning tow and another seventy bucks for Buster's Towing—discount for frequent use—gets Lucky and his gear and his ailing car to Silver Bow Auto. Lucky thumbs a local newspaper in the waiting area, then steps out into the morning air, beside the open service door, stares at the Volvo up on the lift, its dirty underside, the wheels being ratcheted off, then turns to face the highway traffic and reaches into his pocket for his phone.

—

Tara drops the laundry basket with a thump, flops down on the couch, stretches out lengthwise.

"You glad I'm home, Krupa? Company all day is good, eh?" She grabs the phone from the side table. "Looks like your pal Lucky's been calling us. Should we call him back? He might not like what I have to say."

Krupa, hearing Lucky's name stops chewing the end of the rawhide bone, lifts his head, looks from his mat toward Tara with bright-eyed anticipation. As if on cue, the phone's chime tone rings and Krupa's ears perk.

"Hello Lucky. Why're you calling? Thought you were on a vision quest."

Krupa, recognizing a familiar timbre coming from the phone, jumps up and moves to Tara's side, his nose poking toward her hand.

"Butte? Why Butte?" Tara strokes Krupa's ruff. "Buddy who?...Buddy Guy...in Butte! You're kidding. Are you going to work with him?"

Krupa lets out a whimper, followed by a yowly yawn.

"Sh-sh-sh," whispers Tara, fingers at her lips, then rolling her eyes. Krupa yips.

"What? Where are you? By a noisy...You can't hear me? I said WHY PHONE ME FROM A NOISY GARAGE BESIDE A NOISY HIGHWAY?" She pushes the end-call button on her phone.

"Krupa, first he takes off without discussion, then he wants to discuss ON THE FRIGGIN PHONE from hundreds of miles away at a clanking garage beside a roaring highway. Let's go for a walk, get some fresh air."

Krupa's tail wags rapidly as he runs to the door.

—

Four hours later, the axle fixed, Lucky, considerably lighter in his wallet...actually fatter on the credit card, but still determined, aims the Volvo downtown to Hastings Books & Music, the store with the ad in the Butte newspaper, on the off-chance he'll find a Buddy CD, and he does—"Live: The Real Deal" in the used bin.

Once on the I-15, Lucky cranks the speakers loud above the road noise and his financial anxiety and turns the inside of the Volvo into a private concert hall. Buddy wails, but Lucky gives extra attention to drummer Tim Austin, an old-timer who's played with many great blues bands. He's driving the songs with force or subtlety, always just right. Lucky's hands jump on the steering wheel and his left foot plays the offbeat. The miles fly by.

The sun glares from the western quadrant of the sky as Lucky stands by his car on the main drag of Ogden, Utah, stretching and taking in deep breaths of the warm air. His phone buzzes. In the sun's glare he can't see the display of the caller's name. He puts the phone to his ear.

"Tara?"

"Hey Lucky, Stace here."

"Yo, Stace. Long time no see. Seems like only yesterday. How's Butte?"

"Ha-ha. Good here Drummer-boy. Where you at?"

"Beautiful downtown Ogden. Just stopped for a stretch. Cool buildings here. Do you know Peery's Egyptian Theatre? Wow."

"Yeah. Played there. Palace of weird décor, anachronistic, but hip. Listen up, I have an offer from me to you."

"Offer?"

"I need a drummer."

"And."

"You as neat with a beat as you say?"

"Probably better," says Lucky. "You know the difference between a stirred and infinite beat, eh? You're a musician; you know what it means to play your instrument from your heels, not from your wrists. That's what I do."

"OK then. How'd you like to make a u-ee, come and play with the G-tones for a week or maybe two?"

"Gee, Stace, but I'm practically to L.A."

"Ha-ha. You steal a Lamborghini? You could turn around and be back here for a late din."

"I was planning for dinner further down the road."

"You probably dropped a lota scratch on that axle. Need to pay for it?"

"What's up with Garrett?"

"Buddy's drummer's got a stomach flu and they called for Garr to fill in. He's chasing them as I speak. So I need a replacement."

"So you want me to be a fill-in for Buddy Guy's fill-in. Seems a bit... bush."

"Whoa, Lucky. You might have a major league dream, but we make good music here. Keeps people happy. Keeps people paid."

"Right, sorry, Stace."

"I'm offering you a decent gig, pocket change for your pricey stay in L.A."

"Okay, lemme grab a coffee and think about this."

"What's to think about? One half hour, that's all I can give you. I'll even comp your gas if you get here fast. Don't stall. Thirty minutos. You got the number chum?"

"Got it."

Lucky gets back in the car and motors to a diner beside the highway's on-ramp. One way to L.A., the other back north to Butte. He slips into a booth, slides across the red vinyl seat, close to the window. As he sips his coffee he watches the passing traffic, tractor-trailers, motor homes, motorcycles, the whole world seems on the move while he sits still, in a place in between—between what's behind and what's ahead, with a one-eighty crimp now thrown in.

"Man, why do things happen this way?" he mutters. His phone pings and a message pops onto his screen. "Gimme a break, Stace," as he picks it up. Not Stace, but a text from Tara. He reads the last part twice to try and comprehend.

"Don't worry about Krupa & me. Sorry but it's best ths way. I'll leave yr stuff at yr studio in case u need it. No need to call. It's ovr fr us. Good luck."

"Shit," he utters. "Come on," staring at the phone. He punches in Tara's number. Six rings then the voice recording: "Please leave a message."

"Tara...let's not be dramatic...I mean, it doesn't...I'm sorry...I didn't...I don't..." Lucky clicks off.

—

Lucky pushes the empty plate away, wipes the residue of the grilled cheese from his lips, and jabs the number grid on his phone.

"Stace, Lucky here. Tell me a bit more."

"What do you need to know, Lucky? I'm offering opportunity, a gig. You know, I'm taking a chance."

"Me too, Stace. Means I've got to turn around, deviate from my plan, my opportunities south. What's my guarantee?"

"I guess we're both on a slim limb. Never heard you play. What's *my* guarantee? What I say is straight. But I won't be able to keep you longer than two weeks. So then you can crank it for L.A., where, by the way, I've got connections. Might be, as they say, of benefit."

"Okay Stace, you drive a hard bargain. I'm turning around."

"Good lad, you spin, you win.

—

It's dark when Lucky rolls back into Butte, and he heads straight for the Flying J. Stace is in his usual place at the bar.

"Lucky, good to see you. You must have cut it loose to get here so quick. The boys are managing okay tonight without a drummer. Why don't you just sit, listen to the last set, get familiar with the tunes, get yourself ready. Cindy here'll set you a beer and a bite. Rehearsal tomorrow morning, eleven AM"

"Good by me." Lucky tunes into the stage, making mental notes as the band rocks though "Love Me Do," "Dust My Broom," "Heard It Through the Grapevine," and several other golden tunes. They even play a few contemporary ones that Lucky doesn't know, something by Green Day, and their own interpretation of one of those ubiquitous Adele pieces. The bass player and rhythm guitarist driving the beat, with vocals and in-between tambourine licks from the lead guitarist providing some percussive colour. "Not bad at all, even without a drummer," thinks Lucky, "and they cooked with Buddy Guy. I can do this."

On the stool, left foot on the bass pedal, sticks in hand, Lucky looks out into the lounge toward Stace, gives him a slight nod, and eases into the set opener, the famous song by The Band, "The Shape I'm In." As he's playing, Lucky's body takes over. The beat flows from his hands and feet, even his chest, his pelvis. Threads of rhythm lead him. Meanwhile his brain activity moves to another plane. Random thoughts and images glide through—Tara in sunlight, palm trees in L.A., or just a blank—all the while aware of and reacting to the other musicians onstage. Magic moments where everything but the music falls away, where troubles and dilemmas dissolve, where something unexplainable takes over. The drift of melody, the driving, delicious, absorbing beat, the intuitive principles of timing. Exhilarating. A thrust that carries him somewhere beyond the everyday, beyond words, beyond thought and at the same time, beyond and inside the particular song. Lucky launches into backup vocal on the chorus...

"Ooh-ooh, the shape I'm in." He sings with vigour, sings his heart out, his sticks a blur.

—

Tara takes Krupa down by the river and lets him off his leash. The dog sprints and leaps like crazy, exuberance surging from his limbs, releasing all his pent-up energy. After some hard running, Krupa dashes to the edge of the river and wades in, laps up the cool water. He comes out, stands on the bank and shakes, the length of his body wriggling, firing water droplets that sparkle in the evening sun. Krupa begins howling, snout pointing to the sky, like he's singing some ancestral song, a wailing combination of barks and howls, until Tara catches up, cradles his jowls, and tells him to stop.

THE READER'S DREAD

He pauses at the bottom of the page where he is held deliciously on a taut but yielding ribbon of desire, the words rushing to him, embracing and passing through, each one a distinctive taste arousing subtle and varied responses in his body, his being, as his eyes gulp the tiny black morsels, these impulses, mysterious symbols, scratchings, and he cannot stop though he wonders how this could be so, that he consumes so avidly yet is consumed by these things called words, and he wants them, runs headlong at them all the while desiring yet dreading the whiteness that will mark the end of them, the end of his arousal, and he tries to hold, to simply hold on one word, gazing at it continuously to consume it hungrily and fully and repeatedly, while surrounded by the words on all sides though they are nothing but squiggles in his peripheral vision, in fact nothing, nothing at all, yet he would delay forever the conclusion, the release, the end of words, so he holds here, tricking the text, the author, the publisher, hiding here in the shadow of one word among all the words, his eyes, tongue, mind, heart, all concentrated on one group of letters forming one word which begins to dance before him, begins to change shape, begins to slip from his senses toward the nothingness that it is, and he reads it over and over, expresses it on his lips, tries to hold and comprehend the meaning which it is denying him, the typeface blurring, the sound dissolving into white noise, and he wishes to move but a leaden weight overpowers him and the weight is that word which is no longer a word grown to many times its size, grown to suffocate the flow and burn of his desire, grown to become his unlived tale, and his hand struggles, summons its strength against the load of the page, against a great static sleep of dread, lifting the page ever so slightly, revealing barely a hint of the tantalizing stream of waiting words, and he wonders if there's any reason to go on.

ACCIDENTAL CORN

Conrad likes corn, corn on the cob especially. His Dad, Alfred, liked creamed corn but Conrad never has. He found out, though, that creamed corn was safer.

Conrad grew up in a city, but one day—he might have been eight or nine—on a drive in the country with his pal Brian and Brian's parents, they turned off the highway into a family farm, where they were invited to a long outdoor picnic table. These people were strangers to Conrad but he was welcomed nonetheless, and there were other happy visitors too.

Conrad remembers that bright sunny day and a red-and-white checked tablecloth. He can't recall where that farm was, perhaps in the Niagara area, outside Toronto. It was a corn farm. The family put big plates on the table with piles of bright yellow boiled cobs and everyone grabbed cobs and rolled them in butter and salt and dug in. Mouth-watering, sweet, delicious. Conrad ate four or five cobs, maybe six.

That was his first memory of corn, other than the creamed corn that his dad insisted on having with mashed potatoes, the cream's pale liquid seeping, like a slow tide, across the dinner plate and into the other food.

Then there was the more recent, painful, corn episode.

Dad Alfred was a bit of a character, maybe no more eccentric than any dad, but to Conrad it seemed his dad had a conflicted personality. Alfred had a narrow view of the way he thought things should be, but a relaxed attitude toward how others could be—kind of *que sera sera*. Mind you, if someone's *sera* collided with his perception of his personal dignity or principles he'd get feisty, fearless. He'd then exercise a *my way or no way* thing. Like the time his boss told him to initiate a process at the manufacturing plant, something Alfred felt or knew was wrong. He said "No," and marched right up to his boss's boss and told him "Over my dead body." And that was that. Alfred won.

Alfred would never let himself stray from particular tastes and habits: six or seven teaspoons of sugar in a cup of milky tea; creamed corn from a can, not cobbed or nibletted; green vegetables boiled to a pulp; and scouring the newspaper's every detail until he fell asleep in his chair. He loved ice cream too, blobbed into a scooped-out half cantaloupe. Despite oodles of ice cream, Alfred remained lean, never broadening his angular proportions, and his blue eyes stood out over a sharp nose in his narrow face. That was a distinct contrast to Conrad's round visage, but he'd gotten the blue eyes.

Nonetheless, Alfred let Conrad be himself. That was until Conrad's mother, Anne-Marie, prodded his dad to punish him for some perceived misbehaviour. Alfred would not defy Anne-Marie's commands. Conrad couldn't understand that, but forgave his father, even for inflicting underserved punishment with the back of a wooden hairbrush on his palms and not standing up to his mother.

Corn and summer. Conrad loved the association, and he ate lots of corn on the cob late in that season over many years between that farm table and into his retirement, when he was 65. His Dad was by then, gone— on to cream corn nirvana. One summer, five years after Alfred's passing, Conrad was eating a cob in a holiday cabin in a forest on a Gulf Island off Canada's west coast—a truly idyllic setting—sun filtering through enormous cedar and fir trees, ferns bobbing in the warm breeze, butterflies flitting, and birds skittering and calling.

When you hold a cob, one hand on the stem and one hand on the pointy end, of course you get corn juice, but also butter and salt—if you use them—on your fingers, though real sweet corn does not require these additives. One variety of corn is called Peaches & Cream, perhaps because the kernels are a staccato pattern of different shades of yellow, but it tastes like neither peaches nor cream; it tastes like sweet, delicious corn, a taste all its own.

Human ingenuity being what it is, someone invented what Conrad's family had come to call "corn grabbies"—little plastic corn-cob-shaped handles with two metal spikes that were inserted into the ends of the cob, so the eaters could keep their fingers mostly free of the hot cob, and the slathered, oozing, buttery juices that flowed as they bit into the kernels. When Conrad was growing up and eating corn there were no such thing in his family as these grabbies. Part of the pleasure of eating corn on the cob was licking buttered fingers.

Conrad sometimes thought that eating a cob of corn was like typing, his teeth chugging along the cob like the letter slug on the typewriter platen, and the platen shifting with each stroke of the key. And licking his fingers and moving his mouth to another row was like the typewriter's carriage return.

At that dinner, taken in the cabin on the tranquil island, as Conrad chewed along the row of kernels, working his way to the end, he bit into the metal prong of the grabbie that he'd inserted at a bit of an angle. The sound was sharp and grating. A tooth split in half. Pain jabbed his gum. He flung the grabbie across the room toward the sink and shouted, "I hate these fucking things." A spontaneous reaction that shocked not only him, but his dinner companions, his wife, Jenny, and son, Eric. Dental follow-up was required.

After dinner, the corn gone, Conrad said, "I should have stuck to cream corn, like my dad."

His dad, like many of his generation, thought men did not do dishes. He was "a working man" sympathetic to the little guy and a member and supporter of unions for most of his life. If he'd listened to music, he would have loved Woody Guthrie's *Corn Song*, with its calling out of the "rich man," the financial and political manipulative elite. Guthrie sang "Banker man, he take your land," and Alfred believed such narratives, but he also figured those banks were the best investment, much better than the stock market, because "they'll always make money, and if they don't, we're all done for anyway." So he put his money there. He thought of himself as matter-of-fact. He did not express emotions and was easy with silence and entrenchment, which seemed fueled by low-lying anger. Conrad, with time and perspective, deduced that his father's depression was due to that absorbed anger. Yet despite these eccentricities and the inability of his dad to say so, Conrad knew his dad loved him. And Conrad loved in return. How he knew or how that was communicated between them remains a mystery.

One evening, seven years after Alfred's passing, Conrad and family were again at a holiday cabin and Jenny was making dinner, despite having her arm in a cast, having slipped on wet grass and breaking her wrist. Nonetheless she was cooking for Conrad and Eric in the outdoor kitchen on a propane stove. She was cooking corn. She had boiled the water, and to make room for another pan on the stove she had moved the water pot. Conrad knew she was putting on a brave front, beneath a scowl perhaps brought on by pain, so he went to the doorway to see if she needed help. She asked him, as she couldn't manipulate her fingers because of her cast, to strike a match so she could light a burner. Conrad started down the steps not seeing that she had placed that pot of boiled water at the bottom. He bumped the pot and tipped it, spilling the scalding water onto his sandaled foot.

"Fuck, fuck, fuck, Jesus Christ," he screamed and hopped up and down until Jenny told him to stick his foot in the bucket of cold water which was sitting by the outdoor tap. She was a doctor's daughter and knew that would stop the burn from going deeper into the flesh. At that point, with his foot in the bucket and still stinging, Conrad was not thinking of his father, or of corn—he was not thinking of much. He was sobbing.

An ambulance trip ensued, a few kilometres to the dock, then a water ambulance to Vancouver Island, another ambulance van, a Saanich Peninsula Hospital emergency room visit, diagnosis of first and second-degree burns, cleaning, antibiotic ointment, bandaging, and release in the middle of the night. So, he dozed fitfully in the waiting room until time to catch the 6:30 AM ferry back to the island idyll.

Over the next three weeks, in the daily ritual of dressing the wound, Conrad watched his flesh blister and grow raw and bear the pattern of his sandal. He had serious pain, limited activity, and lots of Tylenol. When he had to walk, it was with a limping gait. His foot did not tolerate a shoe well, so he often wore mismatched shoes—a slipper on the burned foot and a runner on the other. He began to use a cane, the one with the gold-coloured handle, given to him by a friend, who used canes just to give a distinguished aspect—a cane Conrad had thought he'd never use. At one treatment, the physiotherapist told him he was using the cane on the wrong side. It seemed counterintuitive to Conrad, but he switched. This, and the limping, and general trauma put his back alignment out resulting in the need for further physiotherapy and massage.

One day, sitting in a doctor's waiting room, he thought, *I should have stuck to creamed corn. Dad was stubborn, but maybe he knew something I didn't—maybe that creamed corn was the safe choice.*

In Alfred's final years, crabby ones, Conrad called him, with affection, "the old creaks." He was stubborn enough at eighty-eight to seal his mouth tight against any nutrient intake—even creamed corn—to bring on his death, prematurely. Alfred left this world bereft, cranky, seething even, without humour...not even of the corny variety. And despite his father's late fury, Conrad was sure that his dad knew he still loved him. That was not enough to save Alfred from his despair, or Conrad from his sorrow.

Conrad had come to understand that Alfred had raged most of his life, but that that anger rode over an underlying sadness and bereavement. Conrad, thinking back on family stories, began to understand that Alfred bore his own father's and his family's despair over the financial abandonment by his wealthy grandfather. Conrad had never gotten all the details but remembered the tale of that boat trip across the Atlantic when Alfred was ten or eleven; the family joyous at Grandfather Hubert's invitation to come to England at his expense and share in his wealth. This would be a reprieve from the hard times Alfred's family was having in the depression. Hubert, the "pig farmer," as Alfred described him, had survived and profited because his product, his good stock of pork, was needed. It was protein for whoever could afford it, and he could charge a premium price.

The rest of the story is even more vague. Conrad recalled hearing different versions and was never sure of the true one. Perhaps it was the family of four kids and two adults that turned up, more rag-tag and needy than Hubert expected; or maybe it was a rejection by Hubert's new wife, unwilling to share her abundance. Whatever it was, the family was forsaken and told to get back on a boat and return to Canada. Conrad could imagine the pain and sorrow of that long last crossing, and on no luxury cruiser—nine endless slow-moving days of dejection, uncertainty, and pain, felt and absorbed into every cell of every member of that now hopeless and frightened family.

Conrad understood how all those emotions, overwhelming for a young boy, were turned inward in Alfred, against himself. Inside he ached and raged but could not curse the way Conrad had, flinging a grabbie, or hopping a boiled-water jig and spewing invective. Alfred's silent rage boiled deep within, at first against, and then later into, "the dying of the day."

One afternoon about eight years after Alfred's death, and one year after Conrad's scalded foot, he was searching cookbooks and websites for an easy recipe. He found one for salmon chowder. Among the ingredients, it called for creamed corn. He made the chowder exactly as directed, though not using canned corn, but boiling the cobs, then slicing the niblets off and creaming them. It was delicious. He thought, *Dad would have enjoyed this.* Conrad imagined his dad even smiling a bit when he told him it was made with creamed corn, the blue in his dad's eyes brightening.

Conrad never uses corn grabbies now, and he has a rule called *Nothing on the Step*, and when ascending or descending, he always looks down before he puts a foot forward. He still loves corn, though he wonders what might have happened, or not, if Jenny had just opened a can that day. But...

"There's nothing like sweet corn on the cob," he says, as he slathers it and licks his fingers.

THE PIANIST

Adam had developed tendonitis in his forearms from playing the piano without warming up his fingers and wrists and by playing too long and holding his arms in the wrong position, which caused the muscles to activate inappropriately until finally the strain became evident in the form of pain that radiated from his wrists to his elbows and prevented him from playing even for a short time so he began to feel distressed and he did not want to fall behind the others in his class, which caused another kind of pain or if not pain then stress and anxiety that became visceral so he resorted to a mental practice imagining his fingers playing on the keys and found he could do this for long periods which helped him keep up and meanwhile he was icing his arms and alternately warming them with a heating pad and also consulting a physiotherapist to learn exercises for his muscles, exercises which he did diligently and, as a result, the discomfort slowly lessened and he was able to return to playing, just minutes at first, then up to ten minutes then twenty then more, which gradually eased his stress and distress until he was fully fluid again and playing for an hour or more at a stretch, thus enabling him to prepare for the duet he was scheduled to perform with his friend Milo, the guitarist, and to return to playing electronic keyboard with his newly formed rock band and so life seemed wonderful until he read of a soldier who had lost both his arms in an explosion in Syria and Adam felt a new kind of anguish born of compassion and he felt gratitude in his understanding that despite setbacks he was most fortunate in a world where others suffered and so he decided to play with new dedication and to devote many of his performances to the injured and underprivileged, realizing that this was all he could do to make a contribution and that he could not alter circumstances for those who suffered but might lift their spirits if even for a few minutes and he tried to remember this every time he encountered a passage that seemed too difficult to learn and thinking "no matter how hard it is I have it easy" and so pressed on with the determination that he had learned from seeing the soldier's struggle which caused him to look at his own fingers and arms as instruments that he shared not just with the piano but also with the soldier without arms and so Adam's arms often felt that they were guided by some other force, by something he could not comprehend, just as he could not explain how the technicalities of the score—the black notes in the staff on the paper—made him move his fingers and body in particular ways to create sounds, that is to say the music he played, which contained mysteries that could cause people to weep or feel exhilaration and transport them onto other planes of perception, as he too himself was transported beyond the physical.

23:44

Summer solstice. In the northern hemisphere, it happens between June 20 and 22, when the North Pole is most inclined toward the sun. The earth's tilt brings the longest day and great light and warmth to everyone above the equator. It gives rise to gatherings and celebrations, festivals and rituals. It is said to be a special and spiritual day and that mystical forces may be unleashed. The effects of the changing angle are felt by all, each in his or her own way. For a few seconds, everything hangs in balance, and then...

—

Roger & Maggie

"We love to play pirate," Roger calls as he hops in and pushes the canoe away from the dock. His partner sits silent and light in the front of the canoe, facing him and the rippling water and the far shore, a pirate hat on her head, her back to the casual observers sunning themselves on the benches by the dock.

"Avast me hearties," he shouts, and a few wave in return as he strokes to back up then turn the canoe in a gradual sweep toward the open water. One voice calls out from onshore, "Bon voyage."

He salutes, and as the canoe arcs, his passenger gazes past him to the watchers. Her expression is placid, serene; the skin of her bare arms, poking from a powder-blue life jacket, is smooth, unblemished, her forearms lifting slightly in her version of a wave, and a response to the gentle breeze whispering across the lake. Roger's strong hands clutch the paddle, and his muscular arms stroke and propel the canoe ahead, brushing his orange vest with a rhythmic rustle. To his companion he says softly, "We're launched, Maggie May." He winks and admires the way her black hat tips jauntily to one side, just the way he'd set it.

"It's a special day. The solstice will just feel like another ruffle in the water."

Her head dips forward in a small nod. Roger turns his glance to the middle of the lake, savouring the tranquil ambience, the chuff of water against the bow, the rhythmic splash of the paddle, the water's mineral smell, and the steady course guided by his adept strokes.

—

Martin, Vicki & Kate

Martin remembers. It was that time fucking Vicki up against the maple tree in the creek valley out behind her parent's house that was the start of Martin's back problems. It was dark, the ground uneven, and Vicki was elevated, her legs around his hips. Awkward. As he thrusted, his eyes lifted from the faint reddish glow of her hair to the June moon, a slivered crescent filtering through the branches overhead. He can almost feel it now, the guttural exhale that rose from his throat toward that moon. But that was decades ago, three to be exact—thirty years ago to the day, that Vicki had insisted on a solstice conjugation, claiming unity with cosmic forces.

Today, his back is killing him. Any movement causes pain. After thirty minutes sitting on the couch watching the news, he tries, tentatively, to stand up, pushing his hands against the soft cushion and falling back, his attention returning to the newscast, its bleak messages, the questions it raises in him. *Are humans incapable of peaceful coexistence?* Pain jabs in his back as he tries to stand again. *Oh Vicki.*

"Oh, oh, Martin, fuck me," she'd squealed as he held her thighs and pushed her against the bark. "Harder." Their panting was louder than the gurgling stream beside them. How, from their brief, intense love, she inhabits him after all those years.

Meanwhile, the pain pills have upset his stomach too. "Take them with food," the pharmacist had said. But he'd ignored that, took them in the middle of the night when he got up to pee. He wonders now if his stomach is ever empty. *Rarely in this country*, he thinks, *which is not the case every-where in this world*. It's all in the news. *The world is fucked, everything off kilter*.

He's gotten up and shuffles stiffly to the phone, his torso tilting to the right. He auto-dials the massage clinic.

"Jocelyn is off today," says the receptionist, "but we have a cancellation with a new massage therapist, Kate. She's very good."

"Must be my solstice luck," he says. "Pencil me in," thinking *Amidst all the bad news, maybe healing forces are at play*.

—

Suzette, Terence & Jim

Suzette had meant to join the oenophile group that Terence belonged to. Whenever Terence and his husband Jim socialized they always presented a wine she'd never heard of—excellent wine at an apparently good price. Terence, always with three days stubble and wearing a ball-cap, the peak turned from his forehead at twenty-three degrees, didn't look like a wine guy as he touted the virtues of membership in the society and in a considerate way boasted about his wine cellar, saying he couldn't drink all the wines he'd purchased since joining the group five years ago. "A Syrah from the Northern Rhone region," or "Etna Rosso from Tenuta delle Terre Nere, the volcanic slopes of Mount Etna in Sicily." Jim tucked his upper lip over his lower and affected a nodding pretense. Suzette could practically hear the rippling currents of the Rhone River, and smell the faint sulphur of the volcanic ash. Her nose wrinkled at this, yet her tongue wet her lips in anticipation.

Suzette, marketing firm office-mate-become-friend of Terence, and now Jim, has, in the past few months, come to enjoy their wit and wine and has offered to help set up and cook for their summer solstice potluck with colleagues. They sit at the shiny white kitchen counter discussing the schedule for the event later that night, and, though it's only mid-day, they're sipping one of the white wines brought up from the wine cellar.

"A German influenced Riesling, from France's Alsace region, a 2008 Éléments from Bott Geyl," says Terence.

"Lovely dress. You look great," says Jim.

"Thank you," says Suzette, a flush rising to her cheeks. She looks down and brushes the light blue fabric at her hips. "I'll need an apron."

"Dry, but you'll taste the fruits, nectarine and pear notes, maybe some floral" Terence says.

"Stony, mineral," says Jim over the low jazz playing in the background.

"Well Jim," says Terence. "Mineral might be apt for a Marlborough Sauvignon Blanc."

"Stony to me," says Jim. Suzette quietly admires Jim's appearance, his dark hair perfectly combed, and his well-fitted, pastel mauve and custard yellow shirt. He's as insistent as he needs to be, responding to Terence's cocksure attitude and verbal precision. Suzette often thinks of them as exemplars of the opposites-attract cliché. Their jibes a burr that rubs or hooks them, and it was sometimes hard to tell which.

She gives Jim a slight wink and rolls the Riesling on her tongue, searching for flavours, for descriptors. Fruit or stone? She has a lot to learn.

"Is that Winton Marsalis?" she asks.

"Good ear," says Jim. "Now let's get to the schedule."

—

Roger & Maggie

Roger paddles toward the centre of the small lake. "Pretty shallow. Think we can catch anything for dinner Miss May?" She is non-committal, seeming to prefer a meditative silence, at one with the gentle bobbing of the boat on the waters. He lifts his rod from the floor of the canoe and gives a slow tug on his leader to ensure that the fly is tightly secured. His eyebrows squeeze together and his tongue moves over his lips as he concentrates and pulls out a few feet of line. He angles the rod over the gunwale and slips out more line behind the canoe, secures the rod's handle and reel under the crook of his knee and begins paddling.

"My Dad taught me that Maggie, rest his fishy soul." The line, threaded through the rod's loops, hums almost inaudibly, the wind strumming the slim fibre. Maggie leans toward him buffed by the increased forward motion of the canoe aimed into the breeze. Roger begins to whistle her namesake tune, Rod Stewart in his head, something less refined through his lips, closer to monotone.

—

Martin, Vicki & Kate

The new therapist extends her hand.

"Kate," she says. Her touch is warm, light.

"Nice to meet you Martin, what's up?"

She's slim and wears dark-rimmed glasses and a short-sleeve blue smock. Martin hesitates, looking at her and thinking, *Her hands look too delicate*, though he has no clear idea what massage-skilled hands should look like.

"Something went wrong in exercise class," he says. "Muscle Pump they called it, but it was mis-pump for me. Sudden painful torque in my lower back."

"Well, let's have a look," she says.

Lying on his stomach, face wedged in the donut cushion at the end of the massage table, he hears Kate squirt lotion and rub her hands together. He closes his eyes. Gentle music flows into the room, a soothing synthesized ripple, like raindrops falling on harp strings. Kate runs her hands over his back, and he begins to feel like putty until she hits a rock-like knot just below the base of his spine and to the left.

"I see," she says. The knotted muscles become targets for her manipulations. She works the upper part of his glutes with her fingers, forearms and elbows. Feels to Martin like she's probing with the end of an axe-handle. Every press on the knots shoots fire through the rest of his body. She rolls her forearms back and forth across the nubs like a barbed steamroller. She digs in, an archaeologist of pain. Martin wheezes, sure that the donut is making permanent circles on his face, and that he'll never walk again. Time becomes measured in those seconds when Kate pauses to change positions for better leverage and he feels brief relief and can hear the raindrop-music again, and more spurts of lotion.

"You okay?" she asks. She digs. He winces, can barely gasp an answer.

"Y-e-s-s."

—

Suzette, Terence & Jim

Terence returns to the kitchen clutching a new bottle of wine. The Riesling bottle sits two-thirds empty. A trumpet solo bleats over the kitchen table. Jim and Suzette are laughing, conspiratorially.

"What's the joke?" Terence asks.

"About eggplant," says Suzette.

"A bit off-colour, off-taste," says Jim. "You had to be there."

"Off-colour?" says Terence. "Aubergine?"

"About a pregnant grape," says Suzette.

"It'd make a full-bodied wine," Jim adds. They all laugh. Terence sets the new bottle on the table.

"Should I open this one?" he asks.

"Not quite yet," says Jim, "It's for later. We need to get to work, but one more sip," moving the snout of the Riesling toward Terence's empty glass. At the same time, Suzette reaches for the new bottle to read the label, and as if some force throws off the direction of her arm by a few degrees, she bumps Jim's hand. Chain reaction. Terence instinctively moves his glass to catch the wine, as Jim tries to re-correct. Cross-purposes. The pour spills with a soft splash onto the table.

"Sorry," says Suzette.

"Sorry sorry," say Terence and Jim, their apologies overlapping.

—

Martin, Vicki & Kate

Martin relaxes a little as Kate pauses to adjust the blanket, exposing Martin's upper back. He'd known there was something else wrong as an ache had persisted in his shoulders for the past few days. He figured it was just the effect of his spine's adjustment to the low back discomfort. Apparently not. Something else on its own. Two knots, in behind his shoulder blades, prove as tender as the ones lower down. Kate works those nubs resulting in more pain. The watery music vanishes from his ears with every application of pressure. He groans, grimaces, tries thinking of something else. The memory of the mix of pain and pleasure. *Oh Vicki. I'd do it again.* Then he thinks back to the news, its pain without pleasure: *Tortured prisoners in repressive regimes.* Lotion spurts near his shoulder and left ear. He wonders, *Does the body eventually go numb to suffering?* Kate digs in.

"Aghh," he exhales, trying to breathe the knot, the pain, out.

—

Suzette, Terence & Jim

Jim blots the spilled wine, then lobs the damp napkin into the waste-basket.

"Two points," he says. "For sure, we'd better not open the Franc yet."

"I'm sorry," says Suzette again, putting her hands on her lap.

"Nobody's fault," says Jim. "It's just wine. We have..."

A jarring noise interrupts, a crystalline avalanche.

"What the..." says Jim. Clattering, shattering glass, a bang, whooshing, up from the basement. For a second they all freeze in position, attention perked.

Terrence leaps from his chair, heads for the basement door. Jim jumps up too and Suzette follows. The odour meets them halfway down the stairs. Fruity, tart and sweet at the same time. Terence opens the door to the wine cellar and the smell wells up; shards of green and white glass clink; bottles, some shattered, some intact, amidst corks, screw-tops, and tumbled shelving, in the pool of pungent liquid soaking into the taupe carpet.

"Oh my god," shrieks Terence.

"Shit," exclaims Jim.

Suzette is silent, trying to understand.

"Jesus," says Terence, as he reaches into the rubble for surviving bottles, one hand on the toppled shelf, trying not to create more instability. "Let's get the good ones out, but be careful of the broken glass."

They form a small chain, Terence passing saved bottles to Suzette who passes them to Jim who takes them into the laundry room and sets them upright on the floor.

"Bloody rack gave way," says Terence. "I took that last bottle from the bottom. I thought gravity and the weight of the bottles would keep it stable. Must have made it top heavy. Should have fastened it to the wall."

"That crossed my mind once, but who would have thought," Jim says in a soft tone that mixes I-told-you-so and disquiet.

"I'm so sorry," says Suzette. She feels uncomfortable, as if she's intruded on some intimate domestic scene.

"It's a bloody nightmare," says Terence.

"A freakin' wine flood," says Jim.

"It's the axis tilt," blurts Suzette, feeling that somehow she'd caused this.

"Pardon?" says Jim

"Take this," says Terence, his voice tight with stress, as he passes Suzette an undamaged bottle. Suzette clutches the bottle as if it were precious, or dangerous, one hand on the neck and the other cradling the bottom. She angles it to the light to read the label. *Chateaneuf-du-Pape Mourvèdre.* She studies the last word—*Mourvèdre*—wondering at the pronunciation. She's suddenly aware of her fuzzy focus, her slowed movements, brought on by the wine consumed and the fumes wafting from the floor.

"Here," says Jim, reaching. Suzette steps closer to him, to avoid the ruddy-pink blemish creeping outward in the pale carpet. She passes the bottle. As he takes it, their hands brush. Jim's face softens for an instant, he smiles. Her hand warms. She wonders what Mourvèdre would taste like.

"Maybe we should cancel," says Jim.

"No, no, we can't," says Terence. "It's Solstice." And with a wry smile and a sigh. "This'll make a great ice-breaker."

—

Martin, Vicki & Kate

Kate says "adhesions in your shoulders," pressing her thumbs just below the left shoulder blade. An involuntary gurgle escapes Martin's chest and throat.

Adhesion? Adhesive? Glue? What does this mean to my shoulders?

"Ahh," he exhales under another attack of the knot, and another. "Uh-h-h-h."

Eventually Kate asks him to turn over onto his back, and begins the treatment's denouement, rubbing his deltoids and carefully stretching his neck, and with a slight lift, gently turning his head. He begins to breathe easier. The music comes back into focus—that ambient, processual, and uncategorizable melody played through watery instrumentation. Almost relaxing.

"There," she says, moving out the door, "take your time getting up."

Martin does take his time, leaning on the table and dressing in slow motion, each movement tentative, testing his body's ability to function anew. Something in him has shifted...his body? His mind? He thinks that maybe he even feels better.

—

Roger & Maggie

The canoe drifts easily in the smooth water. The rod rests on the gunnel, Roger's foot on the grip. A tug hits. A fish? A weed? He grabs the handle and eases the rod's tip into the air, lowers it and winds gently on the reel, pulls up again and lowers and winds. Maggie May is silent. He pulls and winds and pulls hard. Whatever was holding the hook lets go and the line sails into the air. It flies over both their heads and with Roger's reflexive yank the hook rebounds and catches Maggie in the back of her neck.

He shrieks, "Maggie." She tilts forward with the impact of the hook. "Maggie," he shouts again.

She collapses, the pirate hat falling to the bottom of the canoe. A puncture. Air escapes through that small hole in the pinky-beige, silicone flesh of Maggie's neck.

—

Martin, Vicki & Kate

Kate meets Martin as he exits the massage room.

"Yes, adhesions Martin. I suggest a few more treatments."

"Adhesions," he says, but his body and brain are so relaxed from the treatment that he can't even formulate a question.

"I'd like to see you in a week to ten days," she says. "We'll have to break that bound-up tissue down."

His world is rippling, vibrating.

"Yes, thanks Vicki."

"Kate," she corrects.

"Sorry, yes, Kate. I'll make an appointment."

Everything is distant and slowed as he navigates again in the vertical world, moves to the reception desk, gathers his faculties, and leans on the counter for support.

"Happy solstice Martin," Kate calls after him, "Take care."

"Same to you," replies Martin. Then he turns and smiles at the receptionist.

She smiles back and says, "Do you know that we're at the maximum axial tilt toward the sun later today, 23:44 degrees? Then we tip back the other way! We hardly notice. It's awesome, isn't it?"

"Yes...magical they say," a slight note of doubt in Martin's tone.

THE RED STONE

Burton-Brae—who could never find out why his parents had given him this name though his mother said it came to her in a dream, which may or may not have been true—was nonetheless comfortable with it, finally, at this point in his life where he was no longer mocked for such a strange designator the way he had been in school with such taunts as Burnt Hombre, Burping Brain, and Bursting Bra, and in fact he had gained some respect as he'd incorporated himself after law school and taken his as the company name though clients often asked where the other partner was and he'd smile and say he was both of them, which did not seem to affect his business relationships, and on this day as the rain had stopped and the sun had finally come out, he left the office early asking his receptionist to forward only urgent messages by text to his phone as he set off on a walk on the beach to rejuvenate and hoping to sort out a quandary about his relationship with his girlfriend, well, one of his girlfriends, Erena, the short blond German who liked Burton-Brae's name and who was more woman than girl especially when she removed her glasses which made Burton-Brae wonder not about the glasses but about the English language and why *womanfriend* seemed less clear and more awkward than *girl-friend* as a relationship-defining term though neither of these indicated exclusivity the way the terms *fiancé, wife,* and *spouse* did, although these words gave Burton-Brae the heebie-jeebies as did Erena's ultimatum, a kind which seemed to him to only occur in movies—but here it was in real life—and it was that she wanted more commitment from him as he seemed unable to confine himself to only one woman or to make long-term plans with regard to exclusivity, never mind marriage, children and such, which of course Burton-Brae was not alone in, by that meaning that he'd come to understand that many other men also had this fear, though Burton-Brae was reluctant to call it a fear but rather saw it as just a normal state of affairs, at least from his perspective as he was perfectly happy conducting himself this way but Erena had said last night in the midst of a passionate embrace that "enough was enough" and it was "all or nothing" which was not something that—let's just call him BB from here on for efficiency's sake—BB had considered, that is, having nothing with Erena with whom he had to admit he had more than just a passing fancy perhaps something that might possibly be love though he couldn't conceive of exactly what love was, yet he did realize that he would miss Erena, possibly even pine for her if she was not close to him, and he to her, by that not meaning constant proximity but rather closeness in the emotional sense, although that was another thing that made BB nervous, the E-word, but nonetheless he was feeling some discomfort in what he thought of as his soul—because he couldn't be sure where else it might be coming from—this feeling of imminent loss—but there were also Sally and Christina to consider, women who BB was also dating though with less frequency than Erena and with less interest and passion but with definite fun and no ultimatums, which enabled BB the kind of carefree existence that he enjoyed, but he could see that the condition of enjoyment was growing relative at this point, and so as he walked on the beach, gazing out over the waters, he thought about these things and now and again picked up a stone and tossed it to the gentle waves in a kind of mindless action that he hoped might somehow ease his troubled mindless mind and bring a clarity which did not seem to be happening until he bent to pick up an unusually red rock and when he stood up and looked along the beach he was surprised to see someone, *Erena* he thought, coming in his direction and he felt a thrill in his soul, for that was where he thought it emanated from, and in his state of delight and staring hard ahead he stumbled over a chunky rock and fell to one knee on the wet sand just as the woman approached laughing heartily, so he raised his hand and presented her with the stone, which she did not take, as her face became perplexed, and then she smiled and took the stone happily, though she was not Erena, and she threw the stone into the water and said "remember me—Jocelyn, from grade eight—I remember you—you're Burnt Hombre," which suddenly made everything abundantly clear to Burton-Brae as he wished he still had the stone and that Jocelyn had been Erena and he said "please refresh my memory" at the very moment that his phone buzzed with a text from the office.

ARNIE'S WORKSHOP

Arnie, thumbing a carpenter's pencil, walked past his wife Ella, who was cleaning the dinner plates, without a word. He entered his workshop, which was once the double garage, through a doorway off the kitchen.

The grey-white pegboard on two walls, with many hooks for tools was, at one time, full—tools graded by size or shape. Now most hooks hung empty. At the workshop's centre, sat a band saw with a sprinkling of sawdust on its silvery surface and a lathe wreathed with curls of wood. Scattered on the floor were files, pliers, and saw blades, some gleaming, some covered with dust.

The shelves over his workbench supported scarred blue tobacco cans holding screws, and jars of dried varnish that looked like solid molasses, deep brown and gold and opaque, shining in fluorescent light like amber jewellery. Rags, brushes and work gloves hunched here and there like sleeping reptiles. Angled in the corner were two cabinets with drawers, some jammed shut, and some ajar and askew with protruding tools. Arnie maneuvered amidst this debris with casual familiarity, stepping in the bare spots or kicking tools aside.

Out of this chaos, Arnie managed his business, turning out distinctive, well-crafted furniture. Some pieces—a round coffee table of laminated teak, a nineteenth century kneeling bench—would even cause him to whisper, when he finished them, "Beauty."

—

Way back when, a short time into their marriage, Ella had directed her Friday evening energy to the re-ordering of Arnie's workshop. She'd stand

and watch him for a bit, marvelling at his focus as he bent over pieces of wood studying the grain or cutting notches with a fine saw, pencil over his ear, his tongue protruding slightly and tucked in the corner of his mouth. When he finished and went to wash up, Ella stayed, and shelved, hung, and aligned the tools. Arnie, at first, took this as a kindness, and appreciated it. When he was showered and she'd swept, they would hug. In this way their affection was exchanged, not so much with passion, but with a respectful caution that became, simply, a habit.

Ella had hoped that eventually his messy ways would be corrected, that the first-of-week order would take hold. But, over time, the more she cleared up, the more he dropped. After several months, she gave up and gradually she visited his workshop less and less, then rarely, and finally, not at all.

When Arnie could not find a tool in the layers, or in the drawers—a drill bit, a hex wrench, a clamp—rather than look harder, he'd hop in the truck and drive to the hardware store and buy a new one, one that would, of course, eventually find its way into a pile on some surface, in an obscure corner of a drawer, or onto the floor. Seeing him return with a hardware store bag, Ella chastised him.

"You're just keeping the hardware store in business," she'd say with an annoyed frown.

It had not always been that way. Ella had been direct and directive and Arnie was yielding and self-effacing. It was the way each thought they were keeping their emotions in check, keeping the peace.

Ella loved opera, particularly the strong characters and powerful voices, while Arnie enjoyed the quiet of his studio when it was so, or the hum of the power tools when they sung, and there was joy in the expressive work of his hands.

Their hugging habit became a stiff formality, and eventually disappeared.

Despite the chaos of his incubation chamber, at the furniture and craft fairs where he showed and in the specialty stores he supplied, Arnie's handiwork attracted compliments from browsers and shoppers, and sold quickly. Commissions for new pieces rolled in.

At a recent show, he sold one piece—a narrow corner table shelf, five feet high, with three slender, pale birch legs curving from the floor just past the edge of the flat top, a slice of maple burl stained dark—to a silver-haired woman who seemed more refined than the usual craft fair visitor. Her bright paisley scarf and suede ankle boots made Arnie think *fashion designer.* She accepted the nine-hundred-dollar price tag and suggested that she might like to discuss more purchases, with a particular look in mind, a marrying of contemporary elegance and folk tradition. Arnie imagined a kind of Shaker look—clean, balanced lines, subtle style, blonde wood.

"Perhaps I could visit your workshop," she'd suggested. She appeared mature, sophisticated, a bit older than Arnie. He was flattered. His attention bounced between that shaker style and the shaky unbalanced feeling in his stomach.

"Not a good time right now. I have some special projects nearing completion. Not much room in there 'til I'm done."

"Well then," she paused. "Will you deliver the shelf yourself? If so, you can come in to see what's already in place." She smiled. "Corrinne," extending a hand.

"Arnold." He surprised himself by using his formal name, the name his dad preferred. Everyone else called him "Arnie" or "Arn." He jerked his hand from his pocket toward hers. There was a fresh foresty scent about her. Arnie tried to name it...pine? mint? Her clear eyes penetrated his, so he looked down at their hands—his rough and chunky, hers creamy, soft and smooth. But her grip was firm, comfortably firm. Her hand slid slowly from his and reached into her purse. She offered her card. *Corrinne Carleton — Interiors* in tasteful teal type on a pewter grey background. He took the pencil from behind his ear and scrawled his shop number on his note pad and gave it to her.

"I'll deliver the shelf next week and we can settle up then."

"Thanks, Arnold," she said. Arnie nodded. He felt like a boy, receiving favour from a teacher that he had a crush on. But he'd never actually felt anything like that, nor this quiver in his chest. He looked toward his hands. They felt sweaty. He looked up to watch Corrinne's back as she moved on to the next display.

It was a bit of a miracle that Arnie had married, but he had, eighteen years ago, quietly, just the two of them and a commissioner. Now they were both past middle age. He'd met Ella, a petite librarian, when, in a supermarket parking lot, turning into a stall, he bumped her car.

She stared through his car window while he was picking up the oranges that, at his quick stop, had catapulted out of the grocery bag onto the floor of his car. When he got out of the driver's seat and stood, an unhappy woman was looking up at him with an angular face, tight lips, and big, black-rimmed glasses, accentuating her glaring eyes.

A *racoon*, he thought, then glanced at her car door and said "Jeez. I'm sorry. But, hardly a dent."

Her face flushed and her eyes widened, and her voice came out at first with a quaver.

"A dent is a dent and you caused it. You'll have to pay for my repair, sir, in full. I hope you have insurance."

Nobody'd called him "Sir" before. He stared past her fierce look, and felt, for a moment, embarrassed, hesitant.

"Uh, certainly."

Her tone softened.

"Your driver's licence, please."

He reached for his wallet.

—

Arnie, shy and physically awkward, could take no credit for their courtship. It had been Ella who initiated and took control. Early on, as a present, Arnie made her a lovely footstool from cherry-wood, which he had cut to show the dramatic swirling grain.

"You're a talented, handsome man," Ella had said. He seemed solid to her—sturdy, attractive in a boyish way, but dishevelled, needing a bit of management.

Ella had offered comments she thought of as encouraging. "Your woodwork is fabulous, but your workshop..." After a few months of help, her commentary stirred Arnie's resentment. He thought of it as interference. He didn't say much, offering grudging *thank-yous*, but resentment seeped out.

Finally, Ella said, "I give up. I don't know how you work in there. It's masochistic."

Arnie snorted. "Never mind your pop-psychology words." And he continued the tool-dropping and general chaos.

Irritation had become their prime emotional mode, and neither was able to overcome it. Nor could they address or explain it.

—

On the day he was to deliver the corner shelf to Corrinne Carleton, he sat down to lunch with Ella. He felt a jab at his hip. He pulled a small square and tape measure from his pocket and set them on the floor beside his chair.

Afterwards, Ella, listening to opera and cleaning up, put the square and measure in a sideboard drawer. The kitchen and the rest of the house were always neat and clean. It made Arnie nervous.

In his shop he moved a few items around so he could carry the shelf out to his truck in the driveway, intending to stop at the hardware store en route to the delivery. He went back into the house, jangling his truck keys, and Ella, asked, "Where are you off to?"

"Hardware store. Can't find my little square. Then a delivery."

"I see. Would this be it?" she asked, opening the sideboard drawer.

"How'd it get there? Are you hiding my tools?"

"Really?" she said. "Hiding? Misplacing is your specialty. You should get some therapy, Arnie, for your disorder-disorder."

With that he went through the kitchen door to his workshop, dumped a bag of screws onto the floor and kicked them around.

Arnie felt like two people in one skin. Like his hands themselves—skilled in their movements, smoothing and caressing wood, tender or tough as required, but at the same time his flesh was scratched and scarred with splinters, nicks, and chisel slices, and he bore a permanently black thumbnail from repeated hammer-shots that missed the tiny tacks he often held between his fingers. Yet he loved the work, and the tools, despite how they inflicted damage. He loved the feel of them.

A hammer. Maybe the perfect tool, he thought, *the heft, the balance, the power when swung with knowledge and exactitude.* He had several—a small round-nosed metal one, light wood-handled ones, heavy rubber-shafted ones, a variety of sizes of mallets with heads of beech, maple and birch, all scattered about. *And chisels,* he thought, *where would I be without my chisels?* The feel of their handles, the shapes they could make, their keen precision, their bevelled or flat blades, the way they could carve, bring something surprising from the consummation of wood, imagination, and guiding hands. But he could not explain the anomaly—his crazy chaos. So, he ignored it.

Arnie put on a clean shirt, pulled up the shoulder straps on his coveralls, patted his hair and walked quietly past the study where he could hear Ella humming. He stuck a measuring tape and pad and pencil into his pocket and stepped through the shop door. He left quickly, before Ella could chastise him further. On the freeway he glanced at the business card with Corrinne's address, then flipped it onto the dashboard on top of a stack of hardware store receipts. There was more traffic than he thought there'd be at mid-afternoon, and it was hot, but the driver side window-winder handle was missing, so he flicked the fan on full, which blew the dashboard papers into the air. Instinctively he grabbed at them, and in the distraction, he drifted outside his lane. At the loud *honk* he jerked the wheel and let the fluttering receipts be.

He pulled up in front of a stylish apartment building with a doorman who bent to peer in the truck window.

"Trades' parking lot is around back," said the doorman, gesturing to a driveway just ahead. Arnie hesitated—*Tradesman?....Guest?*—then followed the doorman's direction to the rear lot and shipping elevator. He hoisted the shelf from the back of his truck.

He punched her number into his cell phone.

"I'm in the lot, coming up on the shipping elevator." *Classy building,* he thought. There was even a mirror above the control buttons. He checked himself. His coveralls were clean but worn. His face seemed pudgier than he'd thought. He stroked his clean-shaven chin. *I need a haircut.* He clutched the tape measure in his pocket and sucked in his stomach.

Corrinne opened the apartment door wide, stepped back and beckoned him in.

"Thank you for coming Mr. Hamill...Arnold." He maneuvered the shelf into the apartment hallway and set it down, then slipped off his shoes, finally looking straight at her. She seemed taller than he'd recalled.

"Shall I bring the shelf into the living room?"

"Leave it for now. Let's have a look first," beckoning him.

He followed. She was trim but shapely. *Nicely turned*, he thought.

In the living room she turned to him.

"This is it."

The living room was large with windows along one wall, light streaming in past the sheer white curtains, some drawn, some spread.

"I think your shelf will fit well, one of the two empty corners."

She wore fitting stretchy black slacks and a filmy pale lime green blouse, scoop-necked showing her clavicle and above that, her light grey eyes, intense and sparkling. *Like a gin and tonic*, thought Arnie. He suddenly felt dusty, thirsty.

The couch and chairs were white leather, but the other objects—a large, mottled elm bowl, a cluster of painted and stained indigenous masks, bundled and free-standing gnarly branches—were wood, in light and dark shades. Throw-cushions added a flush of sage and mauve. Corrinne moved through the space with the grace of a dancer, one who knows how the body moves and has comfort in it. Arnie felt awkward, out of place. The room, though grand, was softer, more styled, more inviting than he was used to.

"Please sit down." She gestured to the low couch. "We can talk about your fine work. I'm interested in your vision, your talent." She smiled.

As he eased himself onto the couch's edge, he admired the shiny dark walnut coffee table, a crotch-cut with a radiating tendril-patterned grain, on which sat a few glasses and three gleaming bottles—a brown-cast Bailey's, a squarish Jacquiot cognac, and a slim, green-tinted bottle of Pinot Gris.

"Lovely," said Arnie, looking up toward Corrinne who was still standing. "Your table, that is," Arnie added.

"An inheritance from my grandmother. You have a sharp eye."

"Well...wood...you know...I..."

"Yes, you know wood. I've seen the evidence,'" Corrinne smiled again, her eyes directly at Arnie. His eyes darted.

"I've seen what wood, in your skilled hands, can become," she said as she settled onto the couch. His hands fidgeted, drawing her attention.

"You can relax, Arnold," she said. Tea? Or something else?"

—

Arnie arrived home mid-evening, and tentatively opened the door from the garage into the kitchen. The back of his neck was hot and sweat beaded on his forehead. The house was still. An opera, Ella's favourite music, played from the radio. He'd often ask, with a smirk, "Is that Puccini or Zucchini?" Ella hadn't laughed at that in a long while.

"Ella," he called. No response. He walked through the living room and down the hall. His shoes echoed on the hardwood.

"Ella." No reply. *Where was she, anyway?* He knew she'd ask where he had been. He went over to the radio and turned it off and saw the envelope set beside it on Ella's cherry-wood stool. It had an *A* on it in Ella's familiar script. He picked it up, put it in his pocket, and went out the front door to the sidewalk and looked up and down the street. He shrugged and, turning back up the driveway, reached into his pocket, bumping his tape measure, and pulled out the envelope. It opened easily. He stood beside the truck and read.

Dear Arnie,

You didn't talk to me all last week, again. The week before you were surly. It's been like this too long. I've been thinking about this for quite a while now, and tonight you've made it easy by being out. I've gone to stay with a friend. I've got the clothes and things I need for now. You and I can't go on. I'll give you time to adjust then phone you in two weeks to get the rest of my things and to begin to deal with the formalities, logistical, legal, etc. Please don't come by or call me at work. I hope you understand, and perhaps feel relieved.

Ella.

Arnie leaned up against his truck's back bumper. He read the note again.

"Shit."

He stood and walked back to the sidewalk, looking up and down the street. It was the same. The same colours on the houses, the same trees, the same cars in the driveways. But everything was changed. He turned and strode purposefully into the house and through the kitchen to his workshop, banging the door open. He kicked the table he'd been working on and it flipped over. He picked up a hammer, raised his arm, but paused and put the hammer back on the workbench. He turned, went back into the house, flicked on the radio, dialled the opera up loud. An impulse toward his opera jokes formed—Rigoletto, rigatoni—then disappeared. He did not laugh. He auto-dialled Ella's work number, thinking to leave a message, without knowing what that message would be. Halfway through the third ring, he clicked off. The opera crescendoed and faded, the announcer's voice speaking over the last few notes.

"That was *Un bel di, One Beautiful Day* the most popular aria from *Madama Butterfly*, perhaps the best-known opera by the super-star composer, Giacomo Puccini. *Butterfly* premiered in 1904, one year after the car accident which almost killed Puccini and injured his wife and son. Yet he lived another twenty years and completed four more operas. By the time of his death in 1924, he had earned approximately four million dollars from performances of his operas."

"Four million dollars...from opera?" Arnie said this out loud. He clicked the radio off and stared blankly at the books on the shelf above. He scanned the titles, in an unfocussed way. His eyes fell on *The Complete Opera Book*, a thick tome that Ella'd studied, evenings, with her glass of warm water set on her side table. The books were mostly Ella's, except for *Making Model Airplanes with Wood*, a tall slim volume his father had given him when he was twelve, just days before his father's fatal heart attack and Arnold—as his dad had called him—had just begun to make his first model. That airplane and the small tools, glues, and paints, lay scattered and unfinished on Arnie's desk for the next year, until he put them in a box and shoved them under the bed.

Arnie reached for *Making Model Airplanes* and pulled it down. He carried it to his workshop. There he placed it on the stool in front of his only chair, a plain spruce rocker he'd made, where he'd often sit with his pad and draw furniture specs. He straightened up and stared across the workshop, standing stock-still. Then as if coming out of a trance, he moved and up-righted the table he'd kicked over, knelt, and began picking up—a red handled screwdriver, a curved sandpaper block, screws, a small yellow level. They felt like jewels in his hands. He stood and began lining things up, in ordered fashion on his largest workbench. His eyes grew watery and blurred. Arnie wiped their corners with his shirt-sleeve cuff. *Must be the dust*, he thought. Tears welled. A sharp convulsion in his chest jerked his shoulders up then doubled him over. His lungs heaved against his ribs, a guttural sound. His body, beyond his control, clenched, and toppled. He sobbed and sobbed in his nest of tools.

HOMAGE

The *author*—well maybe that's too pretentious a term so let's replace it with *writer* and start over with the *writer*—sat down to answer Italo Calvino's request for "tales consisting of one sentence only, or even a single line," and the writer found himself having fun with the concept and generating a considerable number of such tales, aiming for fifty, or as Spike Lee says in *Mo' Better Blues* "fitty," which he says as the character Giant the gambler and manager who always seems to be wearing clothes too big for him and who gets brutally beat up near the end but otherwise has no role in this story and by that I mean this one right here so back to the main narrative thrust and, to reiterate, the writer of one sentence novels found himself having so much fun that he began to consider the relevance of such work in the context of the great canon of English language—literary novels—fearing that he was not being serious enough to be doing great work but also thinking that somewhere along the way even the writers/authors of famous dark and serious works must have had some fun playing with ideas and rendering them into challenging syntax since, after all, nobody wants to read prose that is boringly structured and totally predictable and why shouldn't a writer even if he wants to or doesn't want to be an author have fun and not address the great themes such as tragedy and betrayal and so on but rather wants to give the reader a series of light and/or deep escapades in reading just to shake up his or her adventure amidst the lines of words and that might even initiate challenges and different expectations in the reader from the usual and yet still provide a kind of unfolding which we might even call plot, and so the writer begins and struggles to keep that narrative flowing in this case with only one character though others are referred to if not developed as fully-fleshed entities for example the reader, other writers, authors, and so on, though in writing seminars one is always reminded that characters have to live and breathe and be visible to the reader so this author will give concession to that principle and say that as he writes he is wearing blue work pants and a green merino long-sleeve light-weight sweater under a black t-shirt from the Gallery of Modern Art Glasgow and is seated and not in any kind of action or crisis other than typing to deal with the rush of words without bringing the sentence to a close in the hopes of satisfying Italo Calvino, who, though, dead is obviously a character too in this narrative—the writer remembering pictures of him with a high forehead due to balding but with sufficient dark hair on the sides to appear distinguished and intellectual and even authorial though the writer wonders if this narrative is the kind of tale Calvino was looking for and what if Italo—if the writer may address him so personally—had seen these stories, each and every one made of one sentence and in some cases of just a single line, what Calvino would have thought and would he have edited these or just enjoyed their reach and might he have ever thought he would be in a story with Spike Lee who was thirty-four years his junior and with a writer who is now eight years older than Calvino was when he died, this writer who may or may not have been to Glasgow but who has responded to Calvino's wish, but of course too late.

INCONCINNITY

Lester looks up from reading. He squirms in his fold-up canvas chair, slips his feet into his sandals, gets up and walks to the edge of the water and wades in up to his knees. *Chilly.* He squints, presses his straw hat firmly on his head and dives—hat, sunglasses, shorts, sandals, book, and all. His nose scrapes the bottom sand, popping his eyes wide open. Tiny fish dart ahead, spring out of view. The buoyancy and cold bite of the ocean water jolt Lester to the surface. He gains his footing, splutters, grabs his sinking sunglasses, his book and floating hat, reaches down for his half-submerged sandals, and he sloshes as fast as he can toward the shore. Trembling, he wince-steps—pebbles and shells jabbing the soles of his bare feet—to his chair, drops his belongings to the sand, grabs his towel and yanks it around his shoulders. With his sandals back on and squishy, he paces in the June afternoon sun, its warmth inching through, easing his shivers.

Lester squints across the strait toward Mount Baker poking above a ribbon of pollution against the pale blue sky. His eyes are watery. The view bubbles. He feels inside and outside his head at the same time.

—

"Remember our island holiday?" Natalie asked as she was weakening. "I wish I could go back."

"Yes, it was...."

"Maybe you'd go there, for me, after...." Her voice a whisper, "I can imagine you there. I remember us...happy."

A chill seemed to come from the overhead vent.

Beside their VW camper with its new avocado green paint job, he and Natalie had sipped margaritas and barbecued steaks and watched the spectacular sunsets over the bay, the fiery reflections on the clouds, the sky mauve then rich blue, darkening and whispering of infinity. They'd loved it. It was one of their better times. Maybe their best.

In the room, with its blipping monitor and sterile light, Lester felt far from that idyll. Natalie exhaled and closed her eyes. Lester took her hand. It felt warmer than his. A slight smiled formed on her lips. He wasn't sure he'd want to go back alone.

—

Lester eases his grip on the towel, pacing, warming, and glances out over the channel. *It* catches a corner of his vision. He stands still, directing his focus beyond the curved beach to a distant edge of the island, at *it*, a black lump punctuating the sky, disproportionate, sitting on top of a tall, skinny protrusion. He stares, perplexed. *I'm on permanent vacation, staring at a lump.*

—

He kicked the front panel of Hunnacker's desk. "Ouch." Pain shot up his shin. "I'm pastured. I've been dumped! I'm a goddamn RETIREE."

"Lester," said Hunnacker, his shiny polka-dot tie with a neat Windsor knot, his hands patting the air to calm. "Please. I don't want you to have a heart attack right here in my office. I'm sorry it's gone this way. It'll look different in a few days, when you realize that you're free. You've been given the golden handshake."

"It's a fist, not a warm palm!" Sweat beaded on Lester's brow. "I've worked hard for this goddam company."

—

"Fuck the handshake." Lester's words burst involuntarily aloud over the beach.

"You alright buddy?" The voice behind startles Lester. He turns to see a dark-skinned, grey-bearded man in a faded red ball cap looking right at him, eyes blue and penetrating.

"Oh...yeah...sure. Just talking to my s-o-b boss."

"Okay. If you say so. Not to intrude, but I saw you jump in. you know, with your clothes on. Thought you were...in trouble...."

"Sorry, no, I'm okay." Lester's face reddens. "Water's straightened me out. Damn cold."

"Yeah, bit early for swimming."

Lester blinks and feels water droplets trickling down his forehead. Self-conscious, he tries to deflect the conversation.

"Do you know what that is over there, that lump on top of that skinny thing?" He points.

"Oh, that. That's a bald eagle on a flagpole. Been sitting there about this time every day lately."

"Oh, that explains. I couldn't figure it," says Lester.

"Yeah, odd sight, isn't it? You know, the pesticides almost wiped the eagles out. Made their eggshells too thin. But since the DDT ban they've rebounded here, and everywhere. Fantastic.... By the way, I'm Kenton." He extends his hand.

"Lester," he says, taking the handshake.

"Your hand's still pretty cold Lester."

"I'm warming up."

"Good. May I invite you to pull your chair over by mine? You can use my binos to watch the eagle, and I've got a little something might help."

"I'm not sure...I just..."

"No pressure. Just a friendly offering. C'mon. Here, I'll grab your chair."

Lester clutches the rest of his belongings and follows, scuffling over the sand and stones.

"Watch out there," Kenton says, pointing near Lester's feet. Scratched into the sand is a radiating pattern, elaborate, like overlapped flower petals, with pebbles and shell bits in the segments. "My handiwork."

"That's...unusual."

"Uh-huh. Mandala. Takes me an hour or more to do. Collect the washed up shells and stuff, draw the shapes, then fill in."

"Wow, nice," says Lester, stepping over the mandala.

"Thanks. All that work, so the tide can come and wash it away."

Lester wiggles the legs of his chair into place beside Kenton under a leaning arbutus tree, the leathery green leaves and orange branches providing shade.

"That's how I feel these days."

"How's that?" asks Kenton.

"Washed away, washed up, my state of being."

"Ebbs and flows, Lester. You never know what the tide brings back," says Kenton, lobbing a stone into the waves.

As Lester settles, he looks at the mandala more closely. The individual petals are monochromatic—pieces all white or all black in each section.

"Intricate," says Lester. "You an artist?"

"I do it for...consciousness. Kind of a mindful focus. Lesson in impermanence. And the differences within singularity." Kenton's blue eyes gleam with a distant vision, then turn to Lester and squint above a cheery grin. "This, though, for fun." Kenton puts a cigarette in his mouth and flicks a lighter, inhales. Offers it to Lester.

"Oh, I thought..."

"Yeah, no ordinary cig, Les. Bambalacha. Cheers." Kenton raises his hand in a casual salute, a flash of his pale palm.

Too surprised to refuse, Lester accepts the joint and takes a drag. It'd been years. The smoke coats his tongue and singes his throat on the way down.

"So what brings you here Lester?" Kenton asks.

"Oh, long story." Lester sucks to hold the smoke in, his voice raspy. "New efficiencies, permanent vacation...loss. How 'bout you?" He coughs, sputtering smoke, passes the joint back.

"Long story too. But here's the précis. Successful R 'n' B musician, singer, keyboardist, bass player, drugs, shot in a bar, lived on the street, lost years, recovery." Kenton inhales, pauses, exhales, looking over the strait. "Been holed up here for almost a decade to get away from the scene. Write a few songs. Look after people's gardens and paths."

"Wow," exclaims Lester, "that's..."

"Just life. I carry on...You carrying on...recovering?"

"I don't know...sort of here for my wife."

"Your wife?"

"Oh, she's not here." Lester's voice lowers. "She passed about a year ago."

"I'm sorry," says Kenton, his tone sincere. He leans and puts his hand on Lester's shoulder.

Lester stares at the incoming tide pushing a brow of seaweed up the beach.

—

Natalie's face was haloed by her silvery hair and her favourite pale lilac pillow, which he'd brought to the hospice. He gazed at her but saw a time-lapse movie—flashing back to her young, fine beauty, refined cheeks and nose, the perfect proportions that attracted him in the first place. Her bright but gentle blue-green eyes, their depth. Then, later, the wrinkles at her eyes' corners, youthful tone giving way to weather and age, the sheen dimming, her visage though, still striking. And then...

He and Nat had not always been so close. There'd been times they'd argued ferociously, their eyes hard, locked. They'd rather have been any-where else than beside each other. And they did split. But they'd gotten through everything—togetherness, youthful poverty, child rearing, sep-aration, reconnection, and eventually, a degree of ease and understand-ing, fewer fights. All along, regardless, she'd believed in him and said so, according no blame.

"You're a good man...in your essence," she'd say, even when they were separated. Maybe it was that sort of thing that created the bond that had remained through it all. It was beyond Lester's ability to explain or understand.

He knew there was little time left for her, but he fought off reality. He'd even said, "When you get better, we'll..." then paused. His tongue pushed against his teeth, his lips set, tight. He looked out the hospice window, then back to her. She'd always been petite, sprightly, yet strong, but in these last days she had become a wisp. A lovely, slight, frail husk. Their hands intertwined, in silence. His words might come out wrong, and speaking seemed that it would put an inappropriate weight in the air, air that was thick and thin at the same time. What could he say—*You're getting smaller; I see you through time; your face is different now...I'm sorry?*

That final afternoon his thoughts tumbled but no words crossed his tongue as her breathing slowed, taken and held, in, out. Suddenly her eyes opened wide, burning, looking right at him, and her hand pulsed. He jerked, leaned toward her.

"You were good for me, my love," he said. *Love*, the word he rarely uttered, but now the only word that seemed right. More words escaped. "Thank you from the bottom of my heart. I am sorry. I'll miss you... I wish...." Natalie let go, lifted her palm toward him. She nodded, her mouth moved, wordless, and she exhaled through smiling lips, inhaled sharply, then let go a soft huff, her last.

—

"Another toke?" Kenton offers. Lester's head, feeling like it's in time-expanding slow motion, swivels slowly toward Kenton's voice.

"Oh, no thanks...I'm way up...buzzed enough."

"Up...down," says Kenton, waving his hand through his exhale of peaty smoke. "Do you know that book...*Been Down So Long*...how does it go? Oh yeah, *Been Down So Long It Looks Like Up To Me*...That's my life."

"I don't know the book, but I get your drift. Down. Yeah. I've been knocked down, left, betrayed...not sure I see the up."

"But you know what they say," Kenton sputters a laugh, "what goes down must come up." He grins.

Lester feels light-headed, silly.

"I think that's backwards," he laughs and reaches for the joint.

"Ah, no, you know what Heraclitus said? He said that the way up and the way down is one in the same." Kenton pauses. "You notice because of the bumps, the knocks...but they're just knocks. Betrayal, yeah, it knocks hard. But you get through it."

"Knocks..." all Lester can muster. The words and the waves on the beach seem to blend in the same rhythm, pulling Lester in their drift.

Kenton continues.

"Been knocked over myself, betrayed once by a buddy who stole my melody for a song, made a big hit. Made me furious, depressed. So one day I snuck into his studio and smashed his guitar. But you know what? It didn't make me feel any better." Kenton's voice trails off with a tone of lament. "I love guitars. That just hurt me."

"But sometimes revenge is...you know...they say...sweet...yeah sweet," says Lester, "and bitter too. My boss, Hunnacker, we were friends...once... used to golf together. I'd..." The scene in Lester's mind is suddenly vivid, green and intense. He watches it for a bit.

"You were saying?" prompts Kenton.

"Oh...yeah...we're out on the course in early fall, me and Hunnacker. Nice day. On a long hole Hunner'd knocked one, on his third shot, into the water hazard. Then he then set up way up the slope from the water, on a level spot, thinking that I wouldn't see because I was on the other side of the fairway. It wasn't the first time. I'd managed, what was it...a two-putt, for five total. On the way to the next tee, Hunnacker muttered, *Four*." Lester reaches for the spliff, takes a drag and carries on, his words mingling with exhaled smoke.

"*F-f-f-four*, I said, *you've got to be kidding.* I practically fell over. Hunnacker just kept walking, looking ahead. *You lying son-of-a-bitch*, I said. Loud too...Yeah, boss or not I called him that. He ignored me, towelled his ball, polished his three iron, set up to tee off. *Fuck you*, I exploded, and stormed off the tee. I hopped..." Lester coughs, hard and dry, "...hopped in my car, drove off, left Hunnacker to finish the round, or not, to hitchhike home, or call his wife, or a cab, or whatever...that was that...I was let go."

"Bru--u--u," Kenton draws out the sound through the cloud of smoke, "--tal."

"Yeah, he turned on me. Didn't stick up for me when the downsizing came."

"Whoa, that's B-A-D bad."

A breeze rattles the leaves overhead. Waves sizzle the beach. Lester and Kenton stare into separate mental drifts. Lester picks up the binoculars to look toward the eagle. He scans to find it, but dark shadows ripple his frame, obscure his view. Chattery voices. He lowers the binos. Five young women amble past him, in shorts or bathing suits, towels over their arms, angling toward a spot on a rocky outcrop closer to the water where they spread their towels on the sun-warmed sandstone.

"More birds," says Kenton. "Fledglings."

Lester smiles, turns the binos back toward the eagle. "Eagle's gone."

"Like the fleeting minutes of our lives." Kenton sighs, exhales smoothly through pursed lips, holding out the joint. "Some days I miss my life of music and the road, the lights, the pals, and you know, the birds. But that's the young me, the young musician. But the old me is content here... Stick around and you might settle too. Wait around for the warm water."

—

After Natalie died, Lester knocked about the house and, while it lasted, his job. Without her he felt like a pinball moving through Jell-O, bumping slow motion from room to room, between alarm clock buzz and backing out of the garage, between emptiness and his work desk. He was angry. He became cranky, abrasive. He wanted to go to work, and when there he wanted to go home. He wanted to take down all the pictures of her and pack them away. He wanted to keep them up and in his view. He wanted her back. He was glad that she hadn't had to witness his dismissal—but she would have supported him, held him. He wanted to be someplace else. He wanted.

—

Laughter and high-pitched happy squeals draw Lester and Kenton's attentions. Shining skin, radiant in the bright sun, the glow unearthly, perfect beauty.

"Some flock," says Kenton. "The spectacular lissomness of youth."

Lester watches them, twitching and jumping as they splash the chilly water and nudge one another to be the first to dive. He raises the binoculars to his eyes to take a better look.

"Gorgeous." He smiles to himself, caught between the present vision and a memory of desire—his own youth, at the swimming pool, the girl-friends, the buddies, the fun, the lack of awareness of their exquisite allure, and the ache beneath it all—a moment that incomprehensibly holds decades in its blink. *Timeless time*, he thinks. And he blinks and lowers the binoculars.

"I was just about to poke you," says Kenton. "Voyeuristic, you know, using the binos to watch."

"I know, but you know what? I was really looking into my past, my young life."

"Wouldn't stand up in court. Time travel is no defense unless it's part of an insanity plea...And anyway your lens must be more powerful than mine if it sees that far."

They both laugh.

"Hey, there might be a song in that." Kenton pauses, then "...I was looking through my binoculars...no, no, how about...looking through the lens of time, back at that young life of mine...."

"Nice," says Lester, "but I get a share of royalties eh." They laugh again, more loudly.

Strolling back to his cabin Lester feels lighter, everything vibrant, in a supple drift.

—

The next day Lester arrives at the beach to find Kenton, his ball cap on backwards, sitting and strumming a guitar.

"I've got a melody for our song, and some more lyrics. Listen to this." A few chords on the guitar and he launches right in, singing, kind of Tal Mahal, yearning, lyrical, and fluid.

"Lookin' through the lens of time
Across the gleaming beach
Gazin' back to that young life of mine
A time way out of reach
To the beauties I've beheld
Mermaids on the rocks
The loves that I have held
The loves that I have lost
All the beauties on the rocks
All my beauties on the rocks"

Lester bursts into applause.

"Amazing!"

"Well, still working on it, but you're in line for a fifty percent share. I'm gonna sell this baby for sure. Maybe to a big name. Might make us rich. Lennon & McCartney look out! "

"Great," says Lester. "I need a new career."

Kenton strikes a match, holds it to the joint's tip.

—

From his deck, leaning at just the right angle, Lester can see the flagpole through a gap between the trees. Sure enough the eagle has returned. It still seems improbable—that pin-thin pole, that clump on top, the imbalance. The *inconcinnity*, his dad's favourite word. Funny it should come to him now, with an image of his dad, remote, analytic, and uncomfortable in his skin. For a few seconds Lester feels his father's gesture in his own, awkward and self-conscious, with a slight tremble, as he reaches for his bevelled glass, the one Natalie'd given him on his sixtieth. Beside it, on the railing, he's set a picture, the one of her sitting on the log, her face bathed in the amber tint of the setting sun.

"Nat." Aloud, his own voice startling him. He cradles the glass, lowers his eyes, looks into the cloudy greenish liquid in the sparkling glass, then gazes up toward the eagle, but not really seeing it, the focus of his stare far inward. His mouth moves almost soundlessly, just a bit of breath, a whisper. He takes a sip then licks the salt from his lips.

SHOOTING POOL

Roslynn bends over the edge of the pool table, her chin low to the cue, the top of her flowered summer dress dipping, her blue eyes focussed, her arm cocked at a right angle directing the stroke, the other arm steady on the green felt, fingers forming a notch the cue slides through in its approach to the white ball which it contacts and sends toward the burgundy solid of the seven ball while in her body, her neck and cheeks to be precise, excitement rises in a flush as line of vision leads beyond the table to the cute young soldier just returned from Bosnia, which he calls by the old name Yugoslavia, leading her to question the veracity of his story, and the seven ball careens from the edge of the pocket as the soldier catches her eyes on him and he winks back and she freezes until her opponent nudges her with his hip wanting to line up his shot or to get her attention, as he thinks she is attractive, though he has no story about returning from anywhere wrongly or rightly-named, so decides to write this tale where he can alter things as he sees fit and can create an outcome favourable to himself in which he sends the soldier back to Bosnia or Yugoslavia or whatever history will finally name it, and he lets himself wink at his desirable opponent while discreetly not staring at her deepening neckline and when he nudges her hip she nudges back and he shoots and sinks the twelve ball and her skin tingles and he feels desire in his fingers and lips and he writes more quickly while wondering what will happen and realizes that he has hooked himself on the eight ball.

BOMBER

He started out complaining, and then moved to guerilla tactics, correcting the errors wherever he found them. It had become his obsession, since seeing, over and over, that signs and other texts represented the plural by putting an incorrect apostrophe before the pluralizing 's.' *Lucky 7's; Haircut's by Austin;* even *Carl's Jr. Charbroiled Burgers,* a complex, mystifying misuse. Did Junior belong to Carl, or were the burgers adolescent and owned, or was the charbroiling done by a more minimal method? As well, there were erroneous absences and presences of apostrophes, even two at once in the local newspaper about a robbery—*Mrs. MacDonalds snatched handbag, it's wallet containing four hundred dollars.* And a variety of other abuses.

He carried pens, markers, and two cans of aerosol paint, white and black—the white to erase, the black to place the apostrophe correctly, or the reverse if need be. With his aerosol paints he could be precise because each can could be set with a narrow tube inserted in the nozzle to direct the spray with fine accuracy. Or he could use the full spray for chunkier corrections. His other tool was his computer, where he would rail on social media against apostrophe errors he'd find on websites and in emails.

Precision. His guiding principle. Even in the part of his hair. Parting hair had fallen out of fashion, but was a fashion he maintained—left side, arrow straight, below the part his dark hair slicked back; and above, the hair combed straight across his skull but with a slight curve toward his forehead. This gave him a kind of 1920s look, or at least that's the number he thought of when grooming and refining the look. "The '20s," he'd say, "even that doesn't have the same meaning anymore. Maybe it's the '50s I'm thinking of, after the wars."

The wars. There is no "after." They continue. He calls his war "the art of apostrophe bombing." That's what he'd write as his occupation any time he had to fill out an official form—"Apostrophe Bomber." Most often, no one would even read it, but sometimes a clerk, suddenly nervous, did ask him what that meant.

"Copy editing," he'd reply to avoid elaboration. That usually ended the conversation, both terms being obscure to most. But he found this more fun than saying "carpenter's helper."

He was working at the new housing development being scraped out of the farmland past the edge of the city, where the fertile land sprouted a new stucco and asphalt paradise. There he schlepped fibreboard, buckets of screws, rolls of poly sheathing, whatever he was ordered to do. His coveralls were clean at the start of each day, as crisp as the part in his hair.

On his way to the site, every day, on the crew bus, he passed beneath the sign hanging from the overpass that announced the development—"Rolling Meadow's Estates." Each time, as soon as the sign came into view, and even though he argued with himself about its ambivalence, about whether meadows could possess estates, he knew it was wrong, and his shoulders tensed and his nape shivered.

"That fucking apostrophe." He raised the error with his boss who shrugged and said, "I'll report it." It had not changed.

Tonight he's stayed in the tool trailer, cleaning up, but really waiting for the cover of darkness. Now under the crescent moon and stars he walks up the roadway onto the bridge above the sign, ready to make the correction. The sign hangs vertically on the bridge face, below the concrete curb and the safety railing. The task requires him to dangle off the bridge railing, one hand on a post and the other operating his spray can—just one, the white, for erasure, all that is required for this correction—while hanging at an angle, mostly upside down. It's a stretch. He's met such challenges before. As he anchors his feet against the concrete edge, leans out and down, he feels his hair lifting...or should we say "dropping away" from his forehead. He'd combed it—after taking off his hard hat at the end of the workday—close to his skull in his preferred style. The hairs are dropping now, due to his upside-down position. The lifting-dropping hair and the resulting lightness and slight pull on his scalp is the momentary sensation that draws his attention, distracts him, and for an instant makes him forget his task, so his hand slips and he plunges head first, dropping into a six metre void between him and the asphalt below.

The author is tempted to end the story here, in a dramatic moment, with a defeat in the apostrophe war, the protagonist falling, and the reader hung in suspense.

By the way, you'll notice now that it was not the Bomber, but the author who inserted the earlier comment: *The wars. There is no 'after.' They continue.* Meanwhile the descent will carry on, but at the author's direction, in slow motion.

The cool night air buffets the Bomber's skin, a sensation created not by a breeze, for the night is calm, but by his descent through that air. His right hand still clutches the paint can, holds it slightly outstretched above his head as it had been when he was preparing to make the correction— well actually, because of his inverted position, it is more accurate to say *below* his head. The other hand and arm extend like a wing and begin to move too in front of his head as if to push the ground away when he gets there. His eyes, now focused on the asphalt below, turn its surface into a lake of black flecks, ten thousand apostrophes rippling in his view.

If this were a James Bond movie, there would be a fast convertible car driven by a beautiful woman—friend or enemy?—her hair, darker than the night and flowing in the wind, this woman racing toward the underpass with perfect timing. But this is a nameless apostrophe Bomber movie-story and so far no other characters have been introduced. Well, his boss was mentioned, but only briefly.

I should have said, earlier, that his name was "Jules." Would that have made a difference? Jules, Apostrophe Bomber.

He's fallen about two and a half metres now and his body is tumbling somewhat, like a diver, all the muscles shifting into an awkward roll. The aerosol can has come loose from his grip and descends at an angle, slightly away from his body, flipping, also in slow motion end over end, its nozzle jammed and spraying an arcing trail of white.

Jules is forty. He's been alone for some time, since his girlfriend left him. "I never really understood her anyway" he would say to himself on evenings alone in front of the television or computer screen. Yet he felt lonely those nights. He'd also say "whatever" and so his bombings took on more importance and frequency. She—Miranda—had been however, extremely patient, and was (is) quite lovely, even with, or perhaps because of, her horn rim glasses and her shapely treadmill-worked legs, but she had her limits. "Jules, I have my limits," she would say. "I'm only human."

But Jules, who had no limits to his obsessions, would reply: "Nonetheless we must take arms against a sea of troubles." He thought he was entertaining and that his issues were of great significance, and Miranda was the only one to whom he could reveal his bombing escapades. It made him feel close to her. So too the fact that they'd met in a Continuing Ed Wednesday evening Shakespeare tutorial.

He'd list for her all the errors he'd seen and say, "It's a war. Of apostrophic proportions." Sometimes she'd laugh and say, "Okay, Jules." But other times she'd cry in exasperation. And Jules, uncomfortable with her emotional displays, would head out into the night.

He sees her face in front of him now. Her glinty brown eyes through the horn-rims, her smiling lips, and realizes her kindness. And he slips right through those eyes toward the blackness.

"I'm going to be my own apostrophe," he thinks, as the pavement approaches to welcome him.

Stop. Rewind. Yes, I know that this is not a film...well, it sort of is as I've moved into filmic allusions and techniques. You see, film—well, it's not even film anymore is it? It's video, or digital imagery—but let's call it film for old-time sake nonetheless...where was I?...oh yes, film. Film, compared to books, seems to have so much more capacity and technique for things like close-up, juxtaposition, flashback, and nowadays for weird angles and not just slow motion, but super, super slo-mo. And drones, and those gravity-defying SteadiCam shots. Then there's the behind-the-scenes glimpses and actor interviews. Just check your DVD versions, especially Blu-Ray, before the technology is obsolete. And as we're not really on film here, but on the page, we won't call it a *rewind*, but a *flashback*.

Jules, despite the rhyme, is no fool. He's worked high structures before. So earlier, before leaning over the rail and out of your sight—because I withheld the moment—Jules had fastened a safety harness around his torso and hooked it to the bridge rail. Hence the lack of need for a gruesome and difficult-to-write description of his body meeting the asphalt and the gory detailed *aftermath*—the smear of blood and the broken bones, and the askew configuration of his limbs. (My errant fingers first typed "aftermash" which was not what I intended, but might have been more accurate). Oh, the happy accident. So, no mash, but a bit of math.

Jules has in fact plunged only a few centimeters over half of the way to the road's surface, about 3 metres and a bit. So, Jules is now suspended, dangling in his harness from the bridge railing, but above the road.

"Aye, there's the rub," he says, spinning from the momentum of the fall and sudden stop. The rub is sharp, a pain in his torso, under the belt, around the bottom of his ribs. The aerosol can clatters to the asphalt. The harness clasp is attached to the tether at his back. His arms can reach around to it, but he cannot manipulate the release, given his weight and the tension on the hook. To say the least, a frustrating and embarrassing position.

Options exist. Miranda, a keenly intuitive woman, opposed to carbon emissions, sensing that something is up with Jules, could bike toward his workplace and see him dangling on the bridge and call the fire department. Or Jules' boss, late at work dealing with schedule pressures, as "time-is-money-and-deadlines-must-be-met-so-cash-can-change-hands," could, on his way home, spot Jules and undertake a rescue with a forklift. Or the aforementioned dark-haired beauty, her long hair coal-black and wind-coiffed, could roll up underneath Jules in her convertible, release and lower him into her bucket seat, and speed away, while eyeing him seductively. Perhaps you can even hear the John Barry musical composition that underscores the scene.

Considering these options, as Jules' body stops spinning and bouncing and becomes almost stationary, hanging slumped over his harness and facing down, heaving for breath, he realizes that none of these scenarios will occur. And anyway, they were my ideas not his. Luckily (or not) there is no traffic on this unfinished roadway. His breath settles, and he manages, for his arms are strong from all his physical labour, to grasp the tether and pull his body vertical and upright, while still hooked on. He climbs up the line, grunting and sweating, back to the bridge railing.

Once atop, he leans over the rail, feeling the cold metal of it through his shirt, and he looks down at the sign and the still-there apostrophe, his failed erasure. He shakes his head, detaches the tether and harness, throws them over his shoulder, and walks along the cloverleaf from the bridge to the road below to fetch his dropped aerosol can. When he gets there, he sees that it has landed nozzle-first and released a blast of white onto the asphalt, in the shape of an apostrophe. He decides to let it be.

He bends, picks up the can and stuffs it into his backpack beside the can of black. He straightens and pats his hair. As he walks, the two aerosol cans bump each other and clink to the rhythm of his steps.

That beat segues to a slowly rising triumphant tune, an excerpt from Gustav Mahler's Symphony #1 in D Major, as the camera angle drops to show Jules tall and illuminated by a single street lamp, walking out of its glow and into the shadowy night as the credits roll. There are no apostrophes out of place in the credit texts. The music cross-fades to the whirr of rubber tires on pavement, then to a slow aerosol hiss as the story dissolves to black, the ambiguity leaving the possibility of a sequel in the reader's mind. After all, the apostrophe war continues. Everywhere.

THE PITCH

"Or even a single line," he said tantalizingly, daring the creator to come up with a solution with words which may or may not be possible even though a painter, specifically Picasso, could make a recognizable shape from a single line, so why couldn't a writer, but how long is a single line and what would it need to encompass, since after all visual art is another matter as a pencil or brush can go anywhere without interruption, without lifting from the surface while words are full of spaces and quirks and *meaning*, but what is *meaning* and what is story or tale, and so the writer has arguably a more complicated structure to deal with, so one way she or he might meet this challenge is by rolling on endlessly and tangentially to create a narrative that will cohere or not and have suspense or momentum or connection, but is that happening here where there seems to be just a pile of words poured out by a writer who is in a sense cheating because there are no epic struggles, no tender moments—well one or two—but no real tales the way one likes to think of these where some kind of human predicament or lesson is demonstrated in a particular time and place which may transport the reader or in some cases cause him or her simply to give up and refuse to read further, which is your prerogative, but does not seem to have happened here as you are reading this and there's not far to go now so why not continue because two, or is it three, characters already seen above may reappear shortly and one presumes that something will be revealed.

IN PARIS, A FOUNTAIN

It has been a while since Sam Beckett has been able to travel, what with the wars, the viruses, his boils and bad teeth. Finally, though, here he is in Saskatoon. It might have been the Irish sounding "oon" that had first caught his attention—the city's name rolled naturally off his tongue; and now there is his play's current production. However, though he'd not been public about it, what took him and holds him now is love, love for Evie-May.

Sam—or Andrew, as he'd occasionally identify himself when he felt a pseudonym necessary—had had relationships—several—magnetic, full of attract-repel dynamics.

"Have I truly loved, top to bottom, soul to soul?" he once asked himself. He knew the answer. He did not know love as such in its most elemental form. Let's just say that he didn't have the best love-modelling as a child. Not a new story.

"Want, not want," as one of his characters said.

Sam thought love involved self-control and resistance. In all his romances he hovered above elemental love. Yes, I know, I've now used that term—*elemental*—twice, though Sam would not think of it that way, not use that word. He was wary with words, careful, mistrusting their inaccuracy, abstraction. He searched for the most authentic, distilled phrases.

"Love," he'd said. "It's a word, a story, a pretend."

But, you see, I'm outside his story and his words so can watch and describe circumstances in a way that he could not, despite his skills at parsing and writing of the human condition. And who, after all, is totally self-aware?

Waiting for Godot is soon to run at Persepolis Theatre and "Mister Beckett" or sometimes "Mister B"—as the director, Anatole, refers to him—is attending every rehearsal and demanding that the actors adhere to his interpretations, and not embellish or improvise.

He had been controlled in his childhood by his mother May's fiery tirades and manipulations at what she called his sloth, her disappointment in him. As an antidote, in his art, he exercises cool control—with parings and boundaries. He loves his work and there he strives for perfection, but often feels, at the same time, his failures. For Sam, as in art, as in love.

Now, you might say "Wait, Samuel Beckett died in 1989." I cannot disagree. Nor can I satisfactorily explain his appearance in Saskatoon, during a pandemic, but I simply offer this story as I know it. Precautions were taken, and necessary travel permissions were acquired.

"No, no, lento, lento...raise your head more slowly" says Mr. B, the tone stern through his mask, bony hand pressing his furrowed forehead. Estragon, rather the actor playing Estragon, lowers his head again. "For the length of one silent deep breath," adds Mister B. And so, rehearsals went. Underneath Sam's sternness was the irritation at the fact that this production would play on an ungodly, distancing computer online platform that has taken over the world as a presentation forum.

"But on this Zoom," he'd said to Anatole, "will the play be experienced? I think it will just be seen...not felt. How can any expression pass through this lifeless, flat screen, these masks?"

Anatole, resolve in his eyes behind his red-rimmed glasses, urged, "You must have faith in the power of your words, Mister Beckett. Perhaps the screen is the proper medium for your bleak landscape."

This only made Sam bleak himself, taut from head to toe.

Evenings are different. No need for the mask, in more than one sense. He softens in the arms of his lover, Evie-May. He grumbles about the rehearsal, then bit by bit lets go of dissatisfactions. He cannot let go all the time, for it is deep in his nature not to do so, and when he does, he feels vulnerable, without defenses, a new and unfamiliar sense. At his most raw, when the feeling of love seems to flow through and outward from him, filling him with discomfort, he yields to tears, despite his efforts to hold them back.

"Where is this coming from?" asks Sam, pulling a tissue from the box in Evie's extended hand. "Some deep well of sadness...la tristesse s'ouvre."

They'd met on her stopover in Paris, her two nights between flights back home to Canada. At her hotel she'd gotten off at the wrong floor and wandered the hall looking for her room. Heading back toward at the elevator, chuckling at her disorientation, she heard a shuffle beside her and turned. A gentleman had appeared, and the residue of her laughter slipped to a smile.

"Est-ce que ça va?" he asked with a hint of odd accent. She fumbled in French, embarrassed.

"Je ne suis pas au bon étage," trying to explain. A slight grin crinkled his sharp cheeks. She sensed that the smile was not common to his gaunt face. It was his blue eyes that shone, unrevealing but penetrating.

Evie-May had slipped past Sam's protective shield when he'd not expected. He was drawn by her vivacity, by her comfortable companionship. Loneliness had been wearing him thin, thinner than even the effect of his stomach troubles. Early on he imagined he'd stay within his walls, walls that he didn't even know he maintained. Well, he did know about them, because they'd been with him all his life. He knew them as detachment. Protective walls. Walls against emotional pain. But the pain had manifested in his body. Demand, control, anger, self-effacement, denial, separation, departure. Boils, tooth pain, indigestion, depression. When he mused over his past, he sensed his containment, though could rarely imagine something different; when he did, he thought it could not be possible for him. As much as he sought isolation, his solitariness caused chronic ache.

Now he clings, cleaved open, by the affection given by Evie-May. He's fallen. Fallen in love as never before. It is like flailing in air, warm, embracing, comforting air. But dangerous, because, what if...? He's become, as his characters, elemental, stripped of pretense, of mask, but more emotional.

For Evie-May, this is new territory as well. Oh yes, she's had her loves, some tumbling her, many staying casual. Mostly they were disappointing. Evie often felt blown by circumstance. And the buffeting aroused her suspicious nature and fed her caution, her fear, her own reluctance. She likes her independence—or thinks she does.

Evie is compassionate and can feel, but holds her feelings at bay, even sometimes from herself. She feels, but contains emotions' intensities; sensitive in relationships, she, in the past, shared herself through desire and amour—yet even then it was guarded. At the point when her guard might break, it would bubble into anger, or blame or excuse, sometimes for good reason and sometimes not. There her liaisons stopped. But here is Sam.

That next day in the hotel's Le Petit Café, Evie-May was sipping a café crème before setting out for a walk, when he came in. Carrying his small espresso cup, he approached and gestured to the chair opposite her.

"Je vous en prie," she said, noticing his warmly toned brown wool jacket, elegant cut, yet casual, though showing wear. He nodded, sitting. She was not unused to such approaches, and while wary, she could never, regardless, fully suppress her smile and inviting charm. They chatted in French—she relishing the chance to use her second language, and his diction was effortless, with what she finally discerned was a slight trace of, perhaps British. She was open with details, while his comments were careful, though cordial. He was struck by her bubbly demeanour and her deep, dark brown, yet bright eyes. He heard of her travels and short stay in Paris; she learned that he was interested in visual art, enjoyed Schubert.

"Ah, *Die Winterreise*, très sombre," said Sam, "et Beethoven, le cycle de lieder, *An die ferne Geliebte*."

He told her his name was Andrew Belis "et je fais un peu d' écriture."

She replied "Evie, Evie Carson," thinking the "May" might sound too folksy.

Self-conscious now of the beret she'd chosen to wear, and adjusting the mauve shawl on her shoulders, she spoke of the music she liked—the jazz singers she'd seen at the club in Saskatoon, her swoon over Kurt Elling, his seductive style, of the painters she knew back home. She did not mention her own love of drawing. When their cups were empty, they agreed to meet in late afternoon at the café for an apéritif.

Evie then had wandered through Luxembourg Gardens stopping long at La Fontaine de Medici. She was exhilarated by the bright orange flowers overflowing their stone pots, stilled by the dark wind-ruffled waters of the pond, and captivated by the statues of the giant Polyphemus—once gleaming in bronze, now turquoised with oxidation—hovering over the lovers Acis and Galatea, rendered in white marble. Galatea cradled by Acis' body, in what appeared as a tender representation of love. But what was the threat of the giant? The figures aroused in Evie, at the same time, romantic fantasy and uneasy disquiet.

Later at the Café, Evie and Andrew continued their conversation, remarking on the fountains, wonderful art in the galleries of Paris, and some of the famous artists and characters. Andrew asked Evie about her unusual French accent and she, unintentionally self-conscious, slipped into English.

"I learned in Canada, mainly in Quebec." She laughed and dropped back to French. "Pardon, ça me gêne un peu."

"No need," Andrew's sudden English startling Evie. She realized then that she should have understood that he wasn't native French, a Parisien. There'd been a Gaelic roll to his speech.

"You have an accent in your accent too," Evie said, a tease in her sparkling eyes.

"Irish," he said, hunching his shoulders.

Evie talked about Canada, even her broken marriage, and Andrew kept shifting the conversation away from personal details to comments on art in Paris. Evie detected, though unstated by him, familiarity with artists they named—Chagall, Duchamp. With their second, then third glass of Chardonnay, Andrew became less reserved, warmed by Evie's outbursts of laughter, her natural theatricality. He confessed that his name was really Sam.

"En effet, je m'appelle Sam, Samuel Beckett. Je suis désolé de vous avoir trompée." He explained his tendency toward privacy and concern that his real name might evoke recognition and unbecoming reaction.

Evie raised her eyebrows, showing a hint of mischief.

"Well, my whole name is actually Evie-May, so I was holding back too, a bit shy, I guess."

They both laughed. She was intrigued and impressed to be conversing in Gaelic-inflected, fluent French, and easy English with this mature, apparently near-famous écrivain whose name she did not recognize. Yet, his small deception unsettled her, despite her own. What other secrets did he hold? Yet, charm, personality, mystery, and curiosity, attracted Evie-May and Sam Beckett to this new acquaintanceship. And there was the magnetic pull of, may I say, *fate*.

As they say, the rest is...well not exactly. There's a gap in the story, though you may be presuming it was tilting headlong for romance. One could say there was some of that, but...there are still miles and minutes... years, to cross. Evie-May would return home, to her work as a teacher and with two daughters to raise. Sam would write, roam, and answer his compelling and fraught artistic callings. Over years, just three early postcard exchanges and later one email connected them across distances. Wistful longings surfaced, then submerged beneath the demands of the days and the ebb of time. They didn't always remember, but they never quite forgot.

Sam, as it turns out, though not knowing at the time, would, a decade after they met, and despite his aversion to travel, and enabled by the lifting pandemic restrictions, head across the Atlantic to deliver a lecture at a prestigious art centre in the Rocky Mountains, several hundred kilometres from Evie-May. So, you see, the story is not yet done.

Though Sam eschewed the new technologies and their self-obsession, he had taken to carrying a cell phone, primarily because of a feeling of distance and disorientation in his new mountain hideout, and to enable quick communication, especially with his ailing brother and aging mother, and with creditable producers and directors interested in his work. The rest he could screen out with caller ID and unfamiliar email addresses. Still, what he felt as a barrage of attention annoyed him.

On his second day in the Rockies, as he was walking, filled with awe, on the shore of Lake Louise, still partly covered by ice but not enough to hide its startling aquamarine colour cupped in the looming mountains, he received an email.

"Are you in Saskatoon. I think I saw you, from a distance, on the street. I was looking out a window and it looked like you. Evie-M."

"Non. Mais j'aimerais bien l'être...wish I was," he keyed impulsively." Memory and imagination fired up.

After Evie-May's "I think I saw you" email, though he was not fully conscious of it, Sam began to wonder how he might find his way to Saskatoon. A plan was not required, as *fate*—yes, that word, that force, again—would play its hand with a call from Anatole Brun at Saskatoon's Persepolis Theatre. Learning that Beckett was in Canada, he extended an invitation.

"I will be in your town in seven days," said Sam's email to Evie. In his mind's eye he could see her—shoulder-length brown hair, slim face and cheeks that lifted and rounded invitingly with her wide smile, beneath those brown-black eyes and that glint of light.

Beckett clears his throat and rises from the row near the back of the Persepolis theatre.

"Didi." Sam moves into the aisle and approaches the stage. "That pause needs to be longer so the silence can be heard and felt. And make your face blank then. Think of nothing!"

It pains him to see his work over-interpreted, or rather to see it represented in a way that is not in his mind. Actors just got in the way. He would perform all the roles himself, if he could, eliminating actors entirely. *How*, he wonders, *can I just put my mind on stage?*

The spring weather in Saskatoon is improving. Underfoot, as Sam walks from the theatre to Evie-May's house a few kilometres away, trickles of water run across the sidewalk between patches of ice. The sunshine casts gleaming gems, crystals amidst the melting snow. Meeting other walkers, they each hesitate then take wide berths, given the virus spike. Sam pulls his overcoat collar to his neck, as the wind, despite the sun, pushes a chill, sharper than the damp Irish cold, into exposed nooks. Anticipation, the thought of an evening with Evie-May, warms his chest.

As I said, "They didn't always remember, but they never quite forgot." That's how Samuel and Evie-May came to be in this story. They never forgot. Why might that be? They knew, but did not know, that each had the power to open the other to new depths and horizons, to a level of life and emotion each had not known, despite relationships—attractions, romances, intimacies, and breakups—they'd stumbled through with others along the way. They were about to embrace something so unfamiliar as to be unimaginable. Hence the distractions, submergence, the tolerated distance, the years, and what appears now, a path, initially hesitant, to claim and commitment.

Earlier I referred to "this story," but, of course I'm not Sam, in pursuit of one story, one perfect story. Nor am I Evie-May, with her aporetic shadow narrative. Still, we, teller and character, sometimes pursue one story and live another and another.

So far, this Sam and Evie bit seems like...what...a fairy tale, or perhaps a romantic comedy.

Wait, there are complications. Most do not merit attention here, but for a few. The problem of language. Each knows it in his or her own way, both beset by conundrum. Evie-May feels, oh she can feel. But her emotions are filtered, only anger spurs her words laid bare. The most tender, she holds to herself, only occasionally offering them. Sam proffers words, though, as in his plays, hesitantly, and distilled, yet in a stream.

Her head on the pillow, her face lit with a tranquil smile, his face propped up on his arm, turns toward her.

"M-my beauty," he says, moved to his core, "Mon amour. I, I'm yours."

They kiss.

Such nervous, earnest declarations of love disturb Evie. She says nothing, but holds him close, and occasionally yields an almost unheard whisper "I love you." This is their dance—dance of expression.

And yes, they dance too, in the literal sense. After the day at the theatre, in Evie-May's living room, the radio pulses with Whitney Houston's voice and throbbing beats–"I Wanna Dance with Somebody." She grabs Sam's hand, pulls him off the couch, lets go and waves her arms over her head, slim fingers fluttering the air; she sways and bumps to the rhythms, inviting him to movement. Such rhythmic abandon is not in Sam's repertoire, in his lank body's reserved stiffness, but with E-M—as he's begun to call her—as enticement and inspiration, and in their private domain, he shuffles and jerks, marvelling at her fluid expressive style, her whole body interpreting the beats and instrumentation, the music flowing through her as he spasms to the song's churn.

"Ce n'est pas, vraiment" Sam catches his breath, "Edith Piaf...*La Vie en Rose.*"

Evie laughs and her shimmer shivers Sam's nape.

"Wrong era, this is '80s stuff," she says, "from my twenties."

When the tempo slows, as if the radio deejay is psychic, with Foreigner's "Waiting for a Girl Like You," Evie and Sam come together and hold close, closer than he'd believed was possible, as close with her body as she knew she could be...barely moving, both enthralled, aroused, and made tender, swept beyond his reserve, beyond hers. Words disappear.

But at times, words combust. Broken, fragmented, disintegrating. Fall as ash.

So, Sam and Evie are left, in their present, because of and despite their pasts and conditionings, to rail and fondle, to shout and whisper, to laugh and weep, to attract and repel. Love and anguish, the entangled knots. Each one, in the worst moments, feeling alone, each wondering. Yet each one wanting to be together, a *we*, not an *I*.

Hence, over time, they heal and cleave to each other. Which brings me back to fate. Such a term may arouse mild doubt or harsh scorn from many. A few believe. Sam and Evie-May, eventually, and above everything else, accepted this particular part of their...shall I say...paths.

They, especially Sam, sometimes try to articulate a complete explanation, trying to render, to fully understand the delays, the marvel of their togetherness and the way it holds them now, no matter what, through dark storms and flowering meadows. And at the same time, Sam realizes the flaw, for as one of his characters says, "saying is inventing" but then contradicts himself. Evie-May hovers, concerned more with being than inventing, sometimes, thirsting for something she cannot define, so she contents herself by drifting, moment to moment. Nonetheless, and despite attempts to articulate, and the resulting wordlessness, as directed by fate, by love, Sam and Evie are inventing a life, surrendering, before realizing they'd done so.

"This is...I don't know how this...c'est comme de la magie, de l'enchantement," says Sam, tears leaking from his eyes' corners. "I thought I knew who I was, but now..."
"Tu es Sam. De la magie?" Evie-May smiles, radiant, "Comme le lapin tiré d'un chapeau, a rabbit from a hat?"
"No, your metaphor, ce n'est pas suffisant. Magique, comme toi et moi."
Such notions make Evie shy, nervous, and she shies away, distracts.
"Let's go look at the fountain," she says, springing from the couch.

Now then, there is a problem in this story. The time-warp. The issue of the characters' unlikely bond. The masks. The problem of story itself—the narrative, the construct, and now this self-referentiality, the obtrusive scribe. You're getting tired of that trope, right? The teller's intrusion, the symbols. But how else to be transparent? Sam and Evie strove to be so, despite their inherent reluctant tendencies, and because of fate. But never mind.

"The fountain?" Sam squints doubtfully. "Are we in Rome? Paris? There's just one fountain here in Saskatoon, le grand bol de soupe."

"But it's a fountain. Water, I want to be near water, the flow," says Evie. "We'll imagine. We can be wherever we want to be."

"Shall we then, à le bol?" He stands and offers his boney hand.

"Superbe idée. Pourquoi pas?" says Evie with a slight bow.

"Certain?" Sam's eyebrows arching, blue eyes widening.

"As can be."

"Enough?"

"Enough," whispers Evie-May with a soft exhale, tilting her head to Sam's shoulder.

"Then, shall we go."

"Allons-y."

Meanwhile you're thinking I forgot about Sam's play. Not the case. At the final rehearsal before the premiere, despite his misgivings and the fact that his preferred actors—Lucien Raimbourg or Patrick Magee— were not on set, in fact are no longer *with us*, Sam managed, after a morning reminder by Evie, to squeeze out a few morsels of generosity.

"Thank you everyone for your efforts to engage with my imagination. No production is perfect, but we strive...my apologies for any demands beyond your capacities. I know the difficulties you work with, the masks, the ever-changing pandemic protocols, the distancing, the absent, screened audience. Just think of this: my play is about, one might say, impediments. Good fortune tonight. Be true and do not rush."

With that, he snatched his overcoat, snapped on his mask and hustled up the aisle and out of the theatre.

"Look, it's working!" Evie steps quickly forward, squeezing Sam's hand. The fountain gurgles, sprays water, droplets caught by the breeze, misting the air, and prisming rainbows. They stop at the edge of the spray, raising their faces to the moisture. She lowers her mask to feel the droplets fully.

"This is almost romantic," she says.

"There is no almost." Sam's reply is wistful and earnest at the same time. "I want this...us...more...closer...every day...I...will not depart...nor will I wait."

The play was well-received. Local and national critics were respectful in their reviews, referring often to Godot's timelessness. The actors were acknowledged for their pacing, the tensions and uncertainties they manifested. Reviewers from away marvelled at the appropriateness of the geographic locale of this production, the spare open spaces of the prairie paralleling the sparse stage set, despite their visit being just virtual.

"It's nostalgia, longing for travel, trying to incorporate the local," says Sam. "It's self-involvement, they're reaching outside the play for relevance instead of inside."

The local radio critic made no reference to this, but did cite, with self-conscious irony, the fact of Godot's first premiere in Paris in 1953 and noting the locally known adage that referred to Saskatoon as "the Paris of the Prairies."

Zoomed audience members, clustered and squished on the participant grid, leaned in, squinted, or stretched back, hands behind their heads. Some turned their gaze off-screen to something more interesting there. Many attended simply by name card, their presence a form of white letters on a black background, a ghostly non-presence. Chats filled the column, the scribes seemingly unaware of the irony of the juxtaposition of their off-the-cuff musings with the poignant evocations of the actors, the playwright's labours of art and craft, and the undistracted immersion required for the full visceral—intellectual and emotional—experience.

Some scanned the grid, searching for the rumoured-to-attend famous playwright himself. His presence was tangible, but he was not to be seen. Some, one assumes, engaged and were affected, perhaps found epiphany.

Evie-May feels a tightness in her chest. The fountain's mist, at first refreshing and sensual, begins to feel like ice. It is not her chest; it is her heart.

Sam pulls closer to her. She yields, but....

"Et alors...maintenant?" queries Sam.

"Yes, let's go," she says.

Sam's arms tighten across Evie's back, his palm at the base of her spine, her eyelids flutter against his neck.

They hardly move.

THE NOTEBOOK MYSTERY

A writer shakes his head to end his daydreaming and sees the open notebook in front of him, so takes up a pencil, then a sharpener, inserts the pencil and twists, watching the thin flakes of wood and slate fall away until the point is thorn-sharp, and then he sets the tip on the paper, reaching with his mind deep into the white clarity where he begins shaping a black mark into a letter of the alphabet then another and another and as words emerge the book's covers begin to close behind him.

Playlist (by story)

Accidental Corn
Woody Guthrie, "Corn Song"

23:44
Dan Gibson, "Dawn in the Valley", on *Songbirds at Sunrise*.
Rod Stewart, "Maggie May."

Arnie's Workshop
Giacomo Puccini, "Un bel di, One Beautiful Day" aria from *Madama Butterfly*.

Bomber
John Barry, perhaps from the film score for the James Bond film *You Only Live Twice*.
Gustav Mahler, "Symphony #1 in D Major."

Camouflage
Bob Marley, "One Love": "Redemption Song"; "Get Up Stand Up"; "Is this Love?"
Beastie Boys, "Check Your Head."
Eric Clapton, "I Shot the Sheriff."

Hammond at the Bluenote
Eddie Taylor, "Looking for Trouble."
Robert Johnson, "Preachin' Blues."
Both performed by John Hammond

Inconcinnity
Taj Mahal, given name Henry Saint Clair Fredericks, & also known for a period as Dadi Kouyate (no particular song).

In Paris, A Fountain
Franz Schubert, "Die Winterreise."
Ludwig van Beethoven, "An die ferne Geliebte."
Whitney Houston, "I Wanna Dance with Somebody (Who Loves Me.)"
Edith Piaf, "La Vie en Rose."
Foreigner, "Waiting for a Girl Like You."

Reason to Believe
The Beatles: "Hey Jude."
Bob Seeger: "Night Moves"
Buddy Guy: "Hoodoo Man Blues," "Sweet Home Chicago." Album, *Live: The Real Deal.*
Garrett & The G-Tones, as performed in the story:
"American Woman," (The Guess Who); "Dust My Broom," (Robert Johnson, recorded in 1936 – also recorded by Elmore James, Canned Heat, & Howlin' Wolf); "Heard It Through the Grapevine," (Gladys Knight & the Pips, Marvin Gaye); "Love Me Do," (The Beatles); "Midnight Hour," (Wilson Pickett).
Lucky Levitt with The G-Tones, as performed in the story: "The Shape I'm In." (The Band)
Unnamed tunes by Adele, & Green Day.

Star Wars
Brian Eno, Album: *Music for Airports.*
Bob Dylan, "Like a Rolling Stone" (*If you ain't got nothin' you got nothin' to lose.*)

The Closets of Time
The Rolling Stones, "Play with Fire."
The Five Satins, "In the Still of the Night."

What Is the Sound of Smoke?
The Platters, "Smoke Gets In Your Eyes" (Jerome Kern composer, Otto Harbach lyricist, 1933.)
The version by The Platters became the number one hit on the U.S. Billboard Hot 100 in 1959. It's been in continual play for eight decades by many artists, and has appeared in novels, film sound tracks, and TV series, and now in Guy and Maddy's story.

Notes & Acknowledgements

The 'shorter' stories are from *Short Novels for People on the Go,* a fifty-part series of one-sentence novels. Those appearing here have been unpublished until now.

—

The author would like to acknowledge the following publishers where these works appeared in earlier forms:
- *Inconcinnity,* appeared in *Grain* Magazine, *Issue v.45.2,* Regina, SK. Winter 2018.
- *What Is the Sound of Smoke* appeared in *What Is the Sound of Smoke?* (Anthology) Mercury Press, Toronto, 2014.
- *The Closets of Time* appeared in *The Closets of Time* (Anthology), TekstEditions Toronto, 2007.
- *Hammond at the Bluenote,* appeared in the collection *Lures,* Mercury Press, Toronto, 1997.

—

Epigraph: from "WHAT'S WRITTEN (DAS GESCHREIBENE)" Translation from German by John Felstiner in *Selected Poems and Prose of Paul Celan,* W. W. Norton, New York, London. 2001. P. 263. (The German: *"wer / in diesem / Schattengeviert / schnaubt, wer / unter ihm / schimmert auf, schimmert auf, schimmert auf?"*)

—

Personal thanks to readers, participants, and editors as follows:

Dave Carpenter for encouragement and constructive comments (*Reason To Believe*); Rosemary Nixon for frank feedback (*Inconcinnity*); Kimmy Beach for perceptive observations (*Arnie's Workshop*); Richard Truhlar and Bev Daurio (Dauforth) for their anthology publication of earlier versions of *The Closets of Time* and *What Is the Sound of Smoke?*); David UU for The Berkeley Horse little books for attention to early *Short Novels*; Karl Jirgens for his (unknowing) guest appearance in *Hammond at the Bluenote*; then to D.K. for her expressive dancing and inspiration for *In Paris, A Fountain,* and for the final polish, en français, I thank Renée de Moissac.

Finally a big embrace to Dave Margoshes for his sharp editorial eye and good-natured encouragement for my narrative eccentricities.

I would like to edit a collection of tales consisting of one sentence only, or even a single line.
— Italo Calvino

A story is what you make of it. Every version is its own.
—Anon

PHOTO CREDIT: ODETTE GREABEIEL NICHOLSON

Steven Ross Smith has published fourteen books of poetry, fiction and nonfiction. He is also an arts journalist, specializing in literary and visual arts. His literary work appears in print, audio and video in Canada, USA, and abroad. He is known for his seven-book poetic exploration *fluttertongue*. Over many decades he's been effective too as a literary activist, on behalf of writers, speaking, teaching, organizing, blogging, editing and presenting. He has lived and written in Toronto, Saskatoon, Banff, Winnipeg, and on Galiano Island. His collaborative chapbook *Table for Four*, created with Winnipeggers Ted Landrum, Jennifer Still, and Colin Smith was published as a limited edition by Jackpine Press in 2020, and the final book in the *fluttertongue* series, coda: *fluttertongue 7*, appeared as well from Jackpine, fall 2021, as a tactile chapbook, whose visualization was a collaboration with Saskatoon designer Brian Kachur. Smith was honoured to serve as Banff Poet Laureate 2019-2021. He was the founding Director of Sage Hill Writing Experience (1990-2008) and Director of Literary Arts at the Banff Centre (2008-2014). Since 2020, he Covid-coped and wrote in Saskatoon after a decade away, until in early 2022, when he fled to Victoria seeking salty waters for his sea kayak.